NEW YORK REVIEW BOOKS
CLASSICS

THE BIG CLOCK

KENNETH FEARING (1902–1961) was born in Oak Park, Illinois. His parents divorced when he was a year old, and he was raised mainly by his aunt. After graduating from the University of Wisconsin in 1924, Fearing moved to New York City where he began a career as a poet and was active in leftist politics. In the Twenties and Thirties, he published regularly in *The New Yorker* and *Poetry* and helped found *The Partisan Review*, while also working as an editor, journalist, and speechwriter, and turning out a good deal of pulp fiction, including pornography. A selection of Fearing's poems has been published in the Library of America's American Poets Project. His 1941 dystopian novel *Clark Gifford's Body*, will appear in the fall of 2006 as an NYRB Classic.

NICHOLAS CHRISTOPHER is the author of fourteen books: five novels, *The Soloist*, *Veronica*, *A Trip to the Stars*, *Franklin Flyer*, and the forthcoming *The Bestiary*; eight books of poetry, most recently *Crossing the Equator: New & Selected Poems, 1972–2004;* and a nonfiction book, *Somewhere in the Night: Film Noir & the American City.* He is a Professor in the School of the Arts at Columbia University.

THE BIG CLOCK

by

KENNETH FEARING

INTRODUCTION BY
NICHOLAS CHRISTOPHER

NEW YORK REVIEW BOOKS, NEW YORK

THIS IS A NEW YORK REVIEW BOOK
PUBLISHED BY THE NEW YORK REVIEW OF BOOKS
1755 Broadway, New York, NY 10019
www.nyrb.com

Library of Congress Cataloging-in-Publication Data
Fearing, Kenneth, 1902–1961.
  The big clock / Kenneth Fearing.
    p. cm. — (New York Review Books classics)
  ISBN 1-59017-181-0 (alk. paper)
  1. Murderers—Fiction. 2. Witnesses—Fiction. 3. Organized crime—Fiction.
4. Women—Crimes against—Fiction. I. Title. II. Series.
  PS3511.E115B5 2006
  813'.52—dc22

                        2005022749

ISBN-13: 978-1-59017-181-3
ISBN-10: 1-59017-181-0

Printed in the United States of America on acid-free paper.
10 9 8 7 6 5 4 3 2 1

CONTENTS

INTRODUCTION

George Stroud is a corporate man. Bland, disgruntled, restless. A former roadhouse owner, racetrack detective, all-night radio broadcaster, timekeeper on a construction gang, newspaper legman, rewrite man, advertising consultant, and, in his own words, "finally—what? Now?" Now he is the editor of *Crimeways*, the investigative crime magazine published by Janoth Enterprises, an empire ruled by the pudgy, pink-faced, strangely listless tyrant Earl Janoth and his icy grand vizier, Steve Hagen. The company, with obviously more than a passing resemblance to the old Time, Incorporated (where Kenneth Fearing toiled for six months in 1942), spins out a slew of magazines, including its flagship, *Newsways*, a business weekly, *Commerce*, and such monthlies as *Sportland, Homeways, Fashions, Futureways*, and a fictional prototype of *People* magazine called *Personalities*.

Stroud never lets us in on why he's had so many different kinds of jobs (it would be interesting to know), but this one is apparently as good as it's going to get for him. And that's not nearly good enough. He tells us more than once that he feels empty, as numbed by routine and repetition as one of Gogol's clerks. It's not clear what exactly he's been emptied of, since he doesn't appear to have possessed much vitality, passion, or creativity to begin with. Unlike Gogol's hapless protagonists, there is nothing feverish or explosive about Stroud. Personally and professionally he has gone stale. Serial adulterer, drunk, he is plagued by irritation, not angst. Even when he finds himself in trouble, he seems too cold and shallow for real anguish.

Janoth Enterprises is housed on the top nine floors of the Janoth Building, which occupies half a New York City block. Stroud refers to it as "an eternal stone deity" with "five hundred sightless eyes...and stone intestines" which seems "to prefer human sacrifices of the flesh and of the spirit, over any other token of devotion." From its capacious lobby to its tightest cubicle, employees plot and scheme, deflect and prevaricate. Treachery and paranoia reign. Power plays, feuds, and vendettas are acted out behind the thinnest of veils. Fearing's prose lights up when he takes on this material. Corporate intrigue (culminating in an unfriendly takeover) seems to interest him more than the intricacies of journalism—or the intrigues of crime, for that matter. For years, Fearing flirted with the American Communist Party, which he may or may not have joined, and all his life remained a dedicated (but by no means doctrinaire) leftist. *The Big Clock* can be read on several levels—murder mystery, psychological study, black comedy—but it is also a quietly subversive take on capitalism and the American corporation.

The concept of the corporate man was big when Fearing published the book in 1946. War veterans (discharged from that ever-expanding postwar corporation, the US military) reenter civilian life, bringing back the insanity, traumas, and psychic wounds of distant battlefields. It is not stated directly, but George Stroud has apparently spent the war years cheating on his wife, not soldiering against the Axis powers. Stroud is not a rebel, not an embittered veteran or damaged war hero (classic characters in noir literature and film), but something far feebler: the wronged man. A victim not so much of his circumstances as his appetites, a man for whom we work up scant sympathy.

Fearing was a serious alcoholic who never sought or achieved long-term sobriety. He died of cancer a month shy of his sixtieth birthday, but it was decades of brutal alcohol consumption and chain-smoking that killed him, one piece at a time. The product of a broken home and chaotic childhood, he started drinking early and hard while attending the University of Wisconsin. Eventually he became a fall-down drunk who suffered frequent blackouts and for long stretches might not bathe, wash his hair, brush his teeth, or change his clothes. It's not surprising that he was notoriously improvident and unreliable, punishing those closest to him with his self-destructiveness. His marriages were predictably disastrous. Unable to hold a job, he churned out pulp novels, many of them soft-core pornography. Of course all of this infected his work. *The Big Clock* may well have been the last good book he wrote; certainly it was the most ambitious and cohesive of his seven novels.

Fearing was born in Oak Park, Illinois, in 1902, three years after the birth of its most famous native son, Ernest Hemingway. Son of a successful Chicago attorney, Fearing had a distinguished lineage that included one uncle who was the first director of the Institute for Advanced Studies at Princeton, another who was the first director of the Rockefeller Institute, and a great-aunt who was the sister of President Calvin Coolidge. For a time, he enjoyed a distinguished career as a poet. He was awarded consecutive Guggenheim Fellowships, won several prizes, and was praised by Edmund Wilson, among others. He wrote six volumes of poetry in all, and his *Complete Poems* was published in 1994. He once said with a kind of bitter pride that he considered himself a freelance writer in the broadest sense, but it is unfortunate that he never managed to insulate his poetic faculty from the wear and tear of hack journalism, pulp writing, and public relations assignments. For a time, writing poetry was coequal with these other, money-chasing pursuits. Finally, though, he could no longer maintain even a modicum of the clarity and precision that serious poetry demands, and it disappeared from his life altogether.

Just as pecuniary references permeate Daniel Defoe's novels (money is mentioned on every page of *Moll Flanders*), and drugs from yage to morphine fuel the fiction of William S. Burroughs, alcohol in all its forms suffuses Fearing's work. George Stroud is a habitué of bars high and low, sleek hotel lounges and the cheapest dives. His drinking is central to *The Big Clock*. It feels as mechanical as his lovemaking, which is usually preceded by a large amount of booze, often to the point of blackout. And it colors all his thinking: while lamenting that events are beyond his control, he never stops trying to control them. He is a fluent liar who vacillates between self-pity and bravado, deluding himself that he is smarter, savvier, than everyone around him. A classic drunk, perhaps he just doesn't care anymore what people think. His wife knows he cheats on her. Not once does he level with her, even when he realizes that the jam he has gotten himself into could destroy her life as well as his.

Fearing makes Stroud's familial relations off-kilter from the start. For one thing, there is the bizarre fact that the three members of the Stroud family all carry the name "George," or diminutives thereof: Stroud is "George," his wife "Georgette," his daughter "Georgia." In their opening scene together, over breakfast, George and Georgette at different times call one another "George." Georgia is also on occasion called "George." Stroud is a humorless protagonist who poses as an ironist; perhaps this toying with his hero's name is Fearing's attempt at dry humor. Like Stroud's overblown storytelling and word games with his daughter at mealtime, it seems extraneous.

Fearing has written a grim book, implausibly plotted, hurriedly concluded, most fascinating when one considers what story must (or might) follow the book's ending. Perhaps for this reason, rather than its plot or style, *The Big Clock* continues to resonate long after we put it down. Why Janoth's business problems and suicide are so tenuously connected to the action of the main story; the reason we never encounter a single policeman or detective, despite the commission of a capital crime; the ease with which Stroud terminates the search of the building just when it seems he will be implicated in Pauline's murder; the fact that Georgette, deep in the novel, out of nowhere, informs the reader that she has known all along of George's infidelities: these are baffling distractions which Fearing allows into his narrative, either by accident or perverse design. In the end, Janoth dies, but Pauline's murder remains unsolved. Hagen, an accessory to murder, is still at large, presumably scheming to secure another cushy executive position. And Stroud—where does he go? To another magazine job, yet another new profession? Or does he simply continue as before—more one-night stands, binge drinking, a continuation of his failed marriage—working his niche under the new management at Janoth Enterprises?

In the story Fearing *has* given us, George Stroud is a corporate man gone dangerously awry. He has cheated, not just on his wife but on his boss, indulging in an extended affair with Janoth's mistress. Pauline Delos is a quintessential ice queen: cold, laconic, shimmeringly blond. After we watch Janoth bludgeon her, the only mystery awaiting a solution is whether or not Janoth will escape punishment (it seems doubtful) and succeed in tracking down and framing the person who saw him at the crime scene. There are other questions, but they are never answered. In the last fateful argument she has in this life, Pauline is accused by Janoth of being a lesbian. He names or identifies five different women with whom she has supposedly slept. She throws back at him that he is gay, illicitly involved (she uses the word "married") with Hagen. We will not find out if these accusations, hurled in the crucible of an impending homicide, are true, and if they are, what bearing they have on Pauline and Janoth's sexual relations. With Stroud, Pauline is decidedly heterosexual. If she is bisexual, Fearing does not indicate it in any other context. But, then, aside from drinking and having sex with Stroud in Manhattan, and taking a road trip to Albany with him to drink, dance, and have sex, we never see Pauline in any other context. She is murdered within minutes of returning from Albany. She doesn't even reappear in a flashback. From then on, the story is Stroud's alone. Some of the other narrators, deftly syncopated, weigh in, but we remain focused on Stroud. Janoth becomes so inconsequential that for two days he is hustled offstage completely, checked into a hospital to escape questioning by the police—and scrutiny by the reader. When he kills himself, we learn of it as Stroud does, by reading a headline in a news kiosk from a passing taxi. Hagen is arguably the most compelling character in the book. He possesses the frigid moral blankness and precise intellect of a Iago. While methodically covering up the murder, he keeps the sloppy and ineffectual Janoth on a short leash. One wishes there had been more of Hagen, who is worthy of a book all his own.

But before we leave Pauline, let's hear again her most interesting utterance: "You are dangerous, George," she says to

Stroud in the midst of their affair. Why, exactly? Because he endangers her position with Janoth? Does that really matter, when Janoth (like Georgette) knows he has already been cheated on many times? Pauline never elaborates on her statement—yet another of the book's loose ends. In fact, neither Stroud nor Pauline nor Janoth is truly dangerous; the most dangerous character in the book is Hagen.

One of the most innovative aspects of *The Big Clock* for a mystery of its time is Fearing's use of multiple narrators, a constantly shifting point of view. He had experimented less successfully with this method in his 1942 novel, *Clark Gifford's Body*, an avant-garde mosaic that employed twenty-three narrators over six decades of scrambled chronology. In *The Big Clock* seven narrators guide us through nineteen segments. Stroud narrates eleven; Janoth three; four minor characters narrate one apiece, as does Hagen. But the most unique element of *The Big Clock* is thematic, not stylistic: its hero, in his capacity as editor of *Crimeways*, finds himself conducting a manhunt in which he is the hunted. Stroud's undermining of his own search becomes the real story. He deflects witnesses, suppresses clues, puts his skills as a liar to good use. But as events become increasingly unmanageable, he coldly lays out the terms of his entrapment: "I thought of hunters stalking big game, and while they did so, the game closed in on its own prey, and with the circle eventually completing itself, unknown disaster drew near to the hunters." This aspect of the book sets it apart from most other mystery novels, carrying us to a more complex existential plateau where we find the works of Georges Simenon, Patricia Highsmith, and Dashiell Hammett. The noir universe is filled with gripping manhunts, but the only comparable one that comes to mind, plot-wise, is the 1950 film noir *D.O.A.*, whose protagonist (another womanizer, who's cheating on his fiancée) has been given a slow poison, discovers he has twenty-four hours to live, and undertakes a frantic, complicated search for his own murderer, which he concludes minutes before his death, entering a police station and declaring that he has a murder to report: his own.

A famous film noir was adapted from *The Big Clock*. For a brief time, the proceeds made Fearing a lot of money—over half a million 2006 dollars. But bad business dealings (he negotiated his own disastrous contract for the film rights) and drunken binges drained the money away just as quickly. The film is a lean, suspenseful mystery, but its hero is not the George Stroud of the novel. In the film, Stroud, though careless, is generally upright, and but for a single all-night bender, sober. The adultery of the novel's hero, the mechanics of his cover-ups, the "semi-residential hotel" where he keeps an "in-town valise" provisioned with clean shirt, razor, etc., is diluted into a single mild indiscretion while Georgette waits to go on the honeymoon she's never had (in Wheeling, West Virginia, no less!). The sex is sanitized altogether. In the film, Stroud never kisses or touches Pauline, much less sleeps with her. (And, somehow, though they barhop together for hours, she remains cold sober, quietly attentive, before covering him with a blanket after he blacks out on her living room sofa.) In 1987, a second film adaptation of the novel, *No Way Out,* is set far from the world of magazine publishing: Stroud becomes a young naval hero; Janoth the US Defense Secretary; Hagen his chief of staff. Pauline Delos is transformed from an erotic femme fatale to a frivolous and flirtatious ex-homecoming queen. The Pentagon replaces the Janoth Building. And there is no Georgette, no Georgia: this Stroud is a bachelor in Washington, DC.

Fearing's original is most notable for its brilliantly effective, supremely modern scenario, the nocturnal hall of mirrors in which Stroud is hunter and hunted, suspect and witness, a man who is seeking to expose one part of the truth while suppressing another. His deep cynicism proceeds from the belief that this is, perhaps, as honest as he, or anyone else, can ever get. And his only salvation lies in the realization that to be truly honest he must be dishonest and vice versa. He is equally prepared to save himself from the gallows with the truth (that Janoth killed Pauline) and also to preserve his tenuous reputation and marriage (claiming he was not her lover) with lies. For Stroud, salvation is not a question of truth—much less spiritual deliverance—but of saving oneself, literally, by any means possible. From Kenneth Fearing, a man who resolutely refused to save himself, this message carries a weight, and poignancy, he perhaps never anticipated.

—NICHOLAS CHRISTOPHER

THE BIG CLOCK

For Nan

GEORGE STROUD I

I FIRST met Pauline Delos at one of those substantial parties Earl Janoth liked to give every two or three months, attended by members of the staff, his personal friends, private moguls, and public nobodies, all in haphazard rotation. It was at his home in the East Sixties. Although it was not exactly public, well over a hundred people came and went in the course of two or three hours.

Georgette was with me, and we were introduced at once to Edward Orlin of *Futureways*, and to others in the group who had the familiar mark upon them. Of Pauline Delos, I knew only the name. But although there could not have been anyone in the organization who hadn't heard a great deal about the lady, there were few who had actually seen her, and fewer still who had ever seen her on any occasion when Janoth was also present. She was tall, ice-blonde, and splendid. The eye saw nothing but innocence, to the instincts she was undiluted sex, the brain said here was a perfect hell.

"Earl was asking about you a moment ago," Orlin told me. "Wanted you to meet somebody."

"I was delayed. As a matter of fact, I've just finished a twenty-minute conversation with President McKinley."

Miss Delos looked mildly interested. "Who did you say?" she asked.

"William McKinley. Our twenty-fourth President."

"I know," she said, and smiled. A little. "You probably heard a lot of complaints."

[3]

A man I recognized as Emory Mafferson, a tiny little dark fellow who haunted one of the lower floors, *Futureways*, also, I think, spoke up.

"There's a guy with an iron face like McKinley's in the auditing department. If that's who you mean, you bet there were complaints."

"No. I was truly and literally detained in a conversation with Mr. McKinley. At the bar of the Silver Lining."

"He was," said Georgette. "I was, too."

"Yes. And there were no complaints at all. Quite the contrary. He's making out quite well, it seems." I had myself another Manhattan from a passing tray. "He's not under a contract, of course. But working steadily. In addition to being McKinley he's sometimes Justice Holmes, Thomas Edison, Andrew Carnegie, Henry Ward Beecher, or anyone important but dignified. He's been Washington, Lincoln, and Christopher Columbus more times than he can remember."

"I call him a very convenient friend to have," said Delos. "Who is he?"

"His earthly alias is Clyde Norbert Polhemus. For business purposes. I've known him for years, and he's promised to let me be his understudy."

"What's he done?" Orlin asked, with reluctance. "Sounds like he materialized a bunch of ghosts, and can't put them back."

"Radio," I said. "And he can put anyone anywhere."

And that was about all, the first time I met Pauline Delos. The rest of the late afternoon and early evening passed as always in this comfortable little palace, surrounded as it was by the big and little palaces of greater and lesser kingdoms than Janoth Enterprises. Old conversation in new faces. Georgette and I met and talked to the niece of a department store. Of course the niece wanted to conquer new territory. She would inherit several acres of the old territory, anyway. I met a titan in the world of mathematics; he had connected a number of adding machines into a single unit, and this super-calculator was the biggest in the world. It could solve equations unknown to and beyond the grasp of its inventor. I said: "That makes you better than Einstein. When you have your equipment with you."

He looked at me uneasily, and it occurred to me I was a little drunk.

"I'm afraid not. It was a purely mechanical problem, developed for special purposes only."

I told him he might not be the best mathematician on earth but he was certainly the fastest, and then I met a small legal cog in a major political engine. And next Janoth's latest invention in the way of social commentators. And others, all of them pretty damned important people, had they only known it. Some of them unaware they were gentlemen and scholars. Some of them tomorrow's famous fugitives from justice. A sizable sprinkling of lunatics, so plausible they had never been suspected and never would be. Memorable bankrupts of the future, the obscure suicides of ten or twenty years from now. Potentially fabulous murderers. The mothers or fathers of truly great people I would never know.

In short, the big clock was running as usual, and it was time to go home. Sometimes the hands of the clock actually raced, and at other times they hardly moved at all. But that made no difference to the big clock. The hands could move backward, and the time it told would be right just the same. It would still be running as usual, because all other watches have to be set by the big one, which is even more powerful than the calendar, and to which one automatically adjusts his entire life. Compared to this hook-up, the man with the adding machines was still counting on his fingers.

Anyway, it was time I collected Georgette and went home. I always go home. Always. I may sometimes detour, but eventually I get there. Home was 37.4 miles, according to the railroad timetable, but it could be 3,740 miles, and I would still make it. Earl Janoth had emerged from somewhere, and we said good-bye.

There was one thing I always saw, or thought I saw, in Janoth's big, pink, disorderly face, permanently fixed in a faint smile he had forgotten about long ago, his straight and innocent stare that didn't, any more, see the person in front of him at all. He wasn't adjusting himself to the big clock. He didn't even know there was a big clock. The large, gray, convoluted muscle in back of that childlike gaze was digesting something unknown to the ordinary world. That muscle with its long tendons had nearly fastened itself about a conclusion, a conclusion startlingly different from the hearty expression once forged upon the outward face, and left there, abandoned. Some day that conclusion would be reached, the muscle would strike. Probably it had, before. Surely it would, again.

He said how nice Georgette was looking, which was true, how she always reminded him of carnivals and Hallowe'en, the wildest baseball ever pitched in history, and there was as usual a real and extraordinary warmth in the voice, as though this were another, still a third personality.

"I'm sorry an old friend of mine, Major Conklin, had to leave early," he said to me. "He likes what we've been doing recently with *Crimeways*. I told him you were the

[6]

psychic bloodhound leading us on to new interpretations, and he was interested."

"I'm sorry I missed him."

"Well, Larry recently took over a string of graveyard magazines, and he wants to do something with them. But I don't think a man with your practical experience and precision mentality could advise him. He needs a geomancer."

"It's been a pleasant evening, Earl."

"Hasn't it? Good night."

"Good night."

"Good night."

We made our way down the long room, past an atmospheric disturbance highly political, straight through a group of early settlers whom God would not help tomorrow morning, cautiously around a couple abruptly silent but smiling in helpless rage.

"Where now?" Georgette asked.

"A slight detour. Just for dinner. Then home, of course."

As we got our things, and I waited for Georgette, I saw Pauline Delos, with a party of four, disappearing into the night. Abandoning this planet. As casually as that. But my thought-waves told her to drop in again. Any time.

In the taxi, Georgette said: "George, what's a geomancer?"

"I don't know, George. Earl got it out of the fattest dictionary ever printed, wrote it on his cuff, and now the rest of us know why he's the boss. Remind me to look it up."

GEORGE STROUD II

Aʙᴏᴜᴛ five weeks later I woke up on a January morning, with my head full of a letter Bob Aspenwell had written me from Haiti. I don't know why this letter came back to me the instant sleep began to go. I had received it days and days before. It was all about the warmth down there, the ease, and above all, the simplicity.

He said it was a Black Republic, and I was grinning in my sleep as I saw Bob and myself plotting a revolt of the whites determined not to be sold down the river into *Crimeways*. Then I really woke up.

Monday morning. On Marble Road. An important Monday.

Roy Cordette and I had scheduled a full staff conference for the April issue, one of those surprise packages good for everyone's ego and imagination. The big clock was running at a leisurely pace, and I was well abreast of it.

But that morning, in front of the mirror in the bathroom, I was certain a tuft of gray on the right temple had stolen at least another quarter-inch march. This renewed a familiar vision, beginning with mortality at one end of the scale, and ending in senile helplessness at the other.

Who's that pathetic, white-haired old guy clipping papers at the desk over there? asked a brisk young voice. But I quickly tuned it out and picked another one: *Who's that distinguished, white-haired, scholarly gentleman going into the directors' room?*

Don't you know who he is? That's George Stroud.

Who's he?

Well, it's a long story. He used to be general manager of this whole railroad. Railroad? Why not something with a farther future? *Airline. He saw this line through its first, pioneer stages. He might have been one of the biggest men in aviation today, only something went wrong. I don't know just what, except that it was a hell of a scandal. Stroud had to go before a Grand Jury, but it was so big it had to be hushed up, and he got off. After that, though, he was through. Now they let him put out the papers and cigars in the board room when there's a meeting. The rest of the time he fills the office inkwells and rearranges the travel leaflets.*

Why do they keep him on at all?

Well, some of the directors feel sentimental about the old fellow, and besides, he has a wife and daughter dependent on him. Hold that copy, boy. This is years and years from now. *Three children, no, I think it's four. Brilliant youngsters, and awfully brave about Stroud. Won't hear a word against him. They think he still runs the whole works around here. And did you ever see the wife? They're the most devoted old couple I ever saw.*

Drying my face, I stared into the glass. I made the dark, bland, somewhat inquisitive features go suddenly hard and still. I said:

"Look here, Roy, we've really got to do something." *About what?* "About getting ourselves some more money." I saw the vague wave of Roy Cordette's thin, long-fingered hand, and discerned his instant retreat into the land of elves, hobgoblins, and double-talk.

I thought, George, you went all over this with Hagen three months ago. There's no doubt about it, you and I are both crowding the limit. And then some.

"What is the limit, do you happen to know?"

The general level throughout the whole organization, I should say, wouldn't you?

"Not for me. I don't exactly crave my job, my contract, or this gilded cage full of gelded birds. I think it's high time we really had a showdown."

Go right ahead. My prayers go with you.

"I said *we*. In a way it involves your own contract as well as mine."

I know. Tell you what, George, why don't the three of us talk this over informally? You and Hagen and myself?

"A good idea." I reached for the phone. "When would be convenient?"

You mean today?

"Why not?"

Well, I'll be pretty busy this afternoon. But all right. If Steve isn't too busy around five.

"A quarter to six in the Silver Lining. After the third round. You know, Jennett-Donohue are planning to add five or six new books. We'll just keep that in mind."

So I heard, but they're on a pretty low level, if you ask me. Besides, it's a year since that rumor went around.

A real voice shattered this imaginary scene.

"George, are you ever coming down? George has to take the school bus, you know."

I called back to Georgette that I was on my way and went back to the bedroom. And when we went into conference with Steve Hagen, then what? A vein began to beat in my forehead. For business purposes he and Janoth were one and the same person, except that in Hagen's slim and sultry form, restlessly through his veins, there flowed some new, freakish, molten virulence.

I combed my hair before the bedroom dresser, and that

sprout of gray resumed its ordinary proportions. To hell with Hagen. Why not go to Janoth? Of course.

I laid the comb and brush down on the dresser top, leaned forward on an elbow, and breathed into the mirror: "Cut you the cards, Earl. Low man leaves town in twenty-four hours. High man takes the works."

I put on my tie, my coat, and went downstairs. Georgia looked up thoughtfully from the usual drift of cornflakes surrounding her place at the table. From beneath it came the soft, steady, thump, thump, thump of her feet marking time on a crossbar. A broad beam of sunlight poured in upon the table, drawn close to the window, highlighting the silverware, the percolator, the faces of Georgia and Georgette. Plates reflected more light from a sideboard against one wall, and above it my second favorite painting by Louise Patterson, framed in a strip of walnut, seemed to hang away up in the clouds over the sideboard, the room, and somehow over the house. Another picture by Patterson hung on the opposite wall, and there were two more upstairs.

Georgette's large, glowing, untamed features turned, and her sea-blue eyes swept me with surgical but kindly interest. I said good morning and kissed them both. Georgette called to Nellie that she could bring the eggs and waffles.

"Orange juice," I said, drinking mine. "These oranges just told me they came from Florida."

My daughter gave me a glance of startled faith. "I didn't hear anything," she said.

"You didn't? One of them said they all came from a big ranch near Jacksonville."

Georgia considered this and then waved her spoon, flatly discarding the whole idea. After a full twenty seconds of silence she seemed to remember something, and asked: "What man were you talking to?"

"Me? Man? When? Where?"

"Now. Upstairs. George said you were talking to a man. We heard."

"Oh."

Georgette's voice was neutral, but under the neutrality lay the zest of an innocent bystander waiting to see the first blood in a barroom debate.

"I thought you'd better do your own explaining," she said.

"Well, that man, George. That was me, practicing. Musicians have to do a lot of practicing before they play. Athletes have to train before they race, and actors rehearse before they act." I hurried past Georgette's pointed, unspoken agreement. "And I always run over a few words in the morning before I start talking. May I have the biscuits. Please?"

Georgia weighed this, and forgot about it. She said: "George said you'd tell me a story, George."

"I'll tell you a story, all right. It's about the lonely cornflake." I had her attention now, to the maximum. "It seems that once there was a little girl."

"How old?"

"About five, I think. Or maybe it was seven."

"No, six."

"Six she was. So there was this package of cornflakes—"

"What was her name?"

"Cynthia. So these cornflakes, hundreds of them, they'd all grown up together in the same package, they'd played games and gone to school together, they were all fast friends. Then one day the package was opened and the whole lot were emptied into Cynthia's bowl. And she poured milk and cream and sugar in the bowl, and then she ate one of the flakes. And after a while, this cornflake down in Cynthia's stomach began to wonder when the rest of his friends were going to arrive. But they never did. And the longer he waited, the lonelier he grew. You see, the rest of the cornflakes got only as far as the tablecloth, a lot of them landed on the floor, a few of them on Cynthia's forehead, and some behind her ears."

"And then what?"

"Well, that's all. After a while this cornflake got so lonely he just sat down and cried."

"Then what'd he do?"

"What could he do? Cynthia didn't know how to eat her cornflakes properly, or maybe she wasn't trying, so morning after morning the same thing happened. One cornflake found himself left all alone in Cynthia's stomach."

"Then what?"

"Well, he cried and carried on so bad that every morning she got a bellyache. And she couldn't think why because, after all, she really hadn't eaten anything."

"Then what'd she do?"

"She didn't like it, that's what she did."

Georgia started in on her soft-boiled eggs, which promised to go the way of the cereal. Presently she lowered the handle of the spoon to the table and rested her chin on the tip, brooding and thumping her feet on the crossbar. The coffee in my cup gently rippled, rippled with every thud.

"You always tell that story," she remembered. "Tell me another."

"There's one about the little girl—Cynthia, aged six—the same one—who also had a habit of kicking her feet against the table whenever she ate. Day after day, week in and week out, year after year, she kicked it and kicked it. Then

[13]

one fine day the table said, 'I'm getting pretty tired of this,' and with that it pulled back its leg and whango, it booted Cynthia clear out of the window. Was she surprised."

This one was a complete success. Georgia's feet pounded in double time, and she upset what was left of her milk.

"Pull your punches, wonder boy," said Georgette, mopping up. A car honked outside the house and she polished Georgia's face with one expert wipe of the bib. "There's the bus, darling. Get your things on."

For about a minute a small meteor ran up and down and around the downstairs rooms, then disappeared, piping. Georgette came back, after a while, for her first cigarette and her second cup of coffee. She said, presently, looking at me through a thin band of smoke: "Would you like to go back to newspaper work, George?"

"God forbid. I never want to see another fire engine as long as I live. Not unless I'm riding on it, steering the back end of a hook-and-ladder truck. The fellow on the back end always steers just the opposite to the guy in the driver's seat. I think."

"That's what I mean."

"What do you mean?"

"You don't like *Crimeways*. You don't really like Janoth Enterprises at all. You'd like to steer in just the opposite direction to all of that."

"You're wrong. Quite wrong. I love that old merry-go-round."

Georgette hesitated, unsure of herself. I could feel the laborious steps her reasoning took before she reached a tentative, spoken conclusion: "I don't believe in square pegs in round holes. The price is too great. Don't you think so, George?" I tried to look puzzled. "I mean, well, really, it seems to me, when I think about it, sometimes, you were much happier, and so was I, when we had the roadhouse. Weren't we? For that matter, it was a lot more fun when you were a race-track detective. Heavens, even the all-night broadcasting job. It was crazy, but I liked it."

I finished my waffle, tracing the same circuit of memories I knew that she, too, was following. Timekeeper on a construction gang, race-track operative, tavern proprietor, newspaper legman, and then rewrite, advertising consultant, and finally—what? Now?

Of all these experiences I didn't know which filled me, in retrospect, with the greater pleasure or the more annoyance. And I knew it was a waste of time to raise such a question even in passing.

Time.

One runs like a mouse up the old, slow pendulum of the big clock, time, scurries around and across its huge hands, strays inside through the intricate wheels and balances and springs of the inner mechanism, searching among the cobwebbed mazes of this machine with all its false exits and dangerous blind alleys and steep runways, natural traps and artificial baits, hunting for the true opening and the real prize.

Then the clock strikes one and it is time to go, to run down the pendulum, to become again a prisoner making once more the same escape.

For of course the clock that measures out the seasons, all gain and loss, the air Georgia breathes, Georgette's strength, the figures shivering on the dials of my own inner instrument board, this gigantic watch that fixes order and establishes the pattern for chaos itself, it has never changed, it will never change, or be changed.

[15]

I found I had been looking at nothing. I said: "No. I'm the roundest peg you ever saw."

Georgette pinched out her cigarette, and asked: "Are you driving in?"

I thought of Roy and Hagen and the Silver Lining.

"No. And I may be home late. I'll call you."

"All right, I'll take you to the station. I may go in for a while myself, after lunch."

Finishing my coffee I sped through the headlines of the first three pages of the morning paper and found nothing new. A record-breaking bank robbery in St. Paul, but not for us. While Georgette gave instructions to Nellie I got into my coat and hat, took the car out of the garage, and honked. When Georgette came out I moved over and she took the wheel.

This morning, Marble Road was crisp but not cold, and very bright. Patches of snow from a recent storm still showed on the brown lawns and on the distant hills seen through the crooked black lace of the trees. Away from Marble Road, our community of rising executives, falling promoters, and immovable salesmen, we passed through the venerable but slightly weatherbeaten, huge square boxes of the original citizens. On the edge of the town behind Marble Road lay the bigger estates, scattered through the hills. Lots of gold in them, too. In about three more years, we would stake a claim of several acres there, ourselves.

"I hope I can find the right drapes this afternoon," said Georgette, casually. "Last week I didn't have time. I was in Doctor Dolson's office two solid hours."

"Yes?" Then I understood she had something to say. "How are you and Doc Dolson coming along?"

She spoke without taking her eyes from the road. "He says he thinks it would be all right."

"He thinks? What does that mean?"

"He's sure. As sure can be. Next time I should be all right."

"That's swell." I covered her hand on the wheel. "What have you been keeping it secret for?"

"Well. Do you feel the same?"

"Say, why do you think I've been paying Dolson? Yes. I do."

"I just wondered."

"Well, don't. When, did he say?"

"Any time."

We had reached the station and the 9:08 was just pulling in. I kissed her, one arm across her shoulders, the other arm groping for the handle of the door.

"Any time it is. Get ready not to slip on lots of icy sidewalks."

"Call me," she said, before I closed the door.

I nodded and made for the station. At the stand inside I took another paper and went straight on through. There was plenty of time. I could see an athlete still running, a block away.

The train ride, for me, always began with Business Opportunities, my favorite department in any newspaper, continued with the auction room news and a glance at the sports pages, insurance statistics, and then amusements. Finally, as the train burrowed underground, I prepared myself for the day by turning to the index and reading the gist of the news. If there was something there, I had it by the time the hundreds and thousands of us were intently journeying across the floor of the station's great ant heap, each of us knowing, in spite of the intricate patterns we wove, just where to go, just what to do.

And five minutes later, two blocks away, I arrived at the Janoth Building, looming like an eternal stone deity among a forest of its fellows. It seemed to prefer human sacrifices, of the flesh and of the spirit, over any other token of devotion. Daily, we freely made them.

I turned into the echoing lobby, making mine.

GEORGE STROUD III

JANOTH ENTERPRISES, filling the top nine floors of the Janoth Building, was by no means the largest of its kind in the United States. Jennett-Donohue formed a larger magazine syndicate; so did Beacon Publications, and Devers & Blair. Yet our organization had its special place, and was far from being the smallest among the many firms publishing fiction and news, covering political, business, and technical affairs.

Newsways was the largest and best-known magazine of our group, a weekly publication of general interest, with a circulation of not quite two million. That was on floor thirty-one. Above it, on the top floor of the building, were the business offices—the advertising, auditing, and circulation departments, with Earl's and Steve Hagen's private headquarters.

Commerce was a business weekly with a circulation of about a quarter of a million, far less than the actual reading public and the influence it had. Associated with it were the four-page daily bulletin, *Trade*, and the hourly wire service, *Commerce Index*. These occupied floor thirty.

The twenty-ninth floor housed a wide assortment of technical newspapers and magazines, most of them published monthly, ranging from *Sportland* to *The Frozen Age* (food products), *The Actuary* (vital statistics), *Frequency* (radio and television), and *Plastic Tomorrow*. There were eleven or twelve of these what's-coming-next and how-to-do-it publications on this floor, none with a large circulation, some of them holdovers from an inspired moment of Earl Janoth's, and possibly now forgotten by him.

The next two floors in descending order held the morgue, the library and general reference rooms, art and photo departments, a small but adequate first-aid room in frequent use, a rest room, the switchboards, and a reception room for general inquiries.

The brains of the organization were to be found, however, on floor twenty-six. It held *Crimeways*, with Roy Cordette as Associate Editor (Room 2618), myself as Executive Editor (2619), Sydney Kislak and Henry Wyckoff, Assistant Editors (2617), and six staff writers in adjoining compartments. In theory we were the nation's police blotter, watchdogs of its purse and conscience, sometimes its morals, its table manners, or anything else that came into our heads. We were diagnosticians of crime; if the FBI had to go to press once a month, that would be us. If the constable of Twin Oaks, Nebraska, had to be a discerning social critic, if the National Council of Protestant Episcopal Bishops had to do a certain amount of legwork, that would be us, too. In short, we were the weather bureau of the national health, recorders of its past and present crimes, forecasters of those in the future. Or so, at one time or another, we had collectively said.

With us on the twenty-sixth floor, also, were four other magazines having similar set-ups: *Homeways* (more than just a journal of housekeeping), *Personalities* (not merely the outstanding success stories of the month), *Fashions* (human, not dress), and *The Sexes* (love affairs, marriages, divorces).

Finally, on the two floors below us, were the long-range research bureaus, the legal department, the organization's public relations staff, office supplies, personnel, and a new phenomena called *Futureways*, dedicated to planned social evolution, an undertaking that might emerge as a single volume, a new magazine, an after-dinner speech somewhere, or simply disappear suddenly leaving no trace at all. Edward Orlin and Emory Mafferson were both on its staff.

Such was the headquarters of Janoth Enterprises. Bureaus in twenty-one large cities at home and twenty-five abroad fed this nerve-center daily and hourly. It was served by roving correspondents and by master scientists, scholars, technicians in every quarter of the world. It was an empire of intelligence.

Any magazine of the organization could, if necessary, command the help and advice of any channel in it. Or of all of them. *Crimeways* very often did.

We had gone after the missing financier, Paul Isleman, and found him. That one could be credited to me. And we had exercised the legal department, the auditing bureau, and a dozen legmen from our own and other units to disentangle Isleman's involved frauds, while one of our best writers, Bert Finch, had taken a month to make the whole complicated business plain to the general public.

We had found the man who killed Mrs. Frank Sandler, beating the cops by three-tenths of a second. This one, also, could be credited to George Stroud. I had located the guy through our own morgue—with the aid of a staff thrown together for the job.

I went straight through my room into Roy's, stopping only to shed my hat and coat. They were all there in 2618, looking tired but dogged, and vaguely thoughtful. Nat Sperling, a huge, dark, awkward man, went on speaking in a monotonous voice, referring to his notes.

". . . On a farm about thirty miles outside Reading. The fellow used a shotgun, a revolver, and an ax."

[21]

Roy's remote, inquiring gaze flickered away from me back to Sperling. Patiently, he asked: "And?"

"And it was one of those gory, unbelievable massacres that just seem to happen every so often in those out-of-the-way places."

"We have a man in Reading," Roy meditated, out loud. "But what's the point?"

"The score this fellow made," said Nat. "Four people, an entire family. That's really big-scale homicide, no matter where it happens."

Roy sighed and offered a wisp of a comment. "Mere numbers mean nothing. Dozens of people are murdered every day."

"Not four at a clip, by the same man."

Sydney Kislak, perched on a broad window ledge in back of Elliot, sounded a brisk footnote: "Choice of weapons. Three different kinds."

"Well, what was it all about?" Roy equably pursued.

"Jealousy. The woman had promised to run away with the killer, at least he thought she had, and when she brushed him off instead, he shot her, her husband, then he took a gun and an ax to their two—"

Roy murmured absently: "In a thing like that, the big point to consider is the motive. Is it relevant to our book? Is it criminal? And it seems to me this bird just fell in love. It's true that something went wrong, but basically he was driven to his act by love. Now, unless you can show there is something inherently criminal or even anti-social in the mating instinct—" Roy slowly opened and closed the fingers of the hand on the desk before him. "But I think we ought to suggest it to Wheeler for *Sexes*. Or perhaps *Personalities*."

"*Fashions*," murmured Sydney.

Roy continued to look expectantly at Nat, across whose candid features had struggled a certain amount of reluctant admiration. He concentrated again on his notes, apparently decided to pass over two or three items, then resumed.

"There's a terrific bank robbery in St. Paul. Over half a million dollars, the biggest bag in history."

"The biggest without benefit of law," Henry Wyckoff amended. "That was last night, wasn't it?"

"Yesterday afternoon. I got the Minneapolis bureau on it, and we already know there was a gang of at least three people, maybe more, working on this single job for more than three years. The thing about this job is that the gang regularly incorporated themselves three years ago, paid income taxes, and paid themselves salaries amounting to $175,000 while they were laying their plans and making preparations for the hold-up. Their funds went through the bank they had in mind, and it's believed they had several full-dress rehearsals before yesterday, right on the spot. A couple of the guards had even been trained, innocently it's believed, to act as their extras. One of them got paid off with a bullet in the leg."

Nat stopped and Roy appeared to gaze through him, a pinch of a frown balancing itself delicately against the curiosity in his blue, tolerant eyes.

"Figures again," he delicately judged. "What is the difference whether it is a half million, half a thousand, or just half a dollar? Three years, three months, or three minutes? Three criminals, or three hundred? What makes it so significant that it must be featured by us?"

"The technical angle, don't you think?" suggested Wyckoff. "Staying within the law while they laid the groundwork. Those rehearsals. Working all that time right through the bank. When you think of it, Roy, why, no bank or business in the world is immune to a gang with sufficient patience, resources, and brains. Here's the last word in criminal technique, matching business methods against business methods. Hell, give enough people enough time and enough money and brains, and eventually they could take Fort Knox."

"Exactly," said Roy. "And is that new? Attack catching up with defense, defense overtaking attack, that is the whole history of crime. We have covered the essential characteristics of this very story, in its various guises, many times before—too many. I can't see much in that for us. We'll give it two or three paragraphs in *Crime Wavelets*. 'Sober, hard-working thugs invest $175,000, three years of toil, to stage a bank robbery. Earn themselves a profit of $325,000, net.' At three men working for three years," he calculated, "that amounts to something over thirty-six thousand a year each. Yes. 'This modest wage, incommensurate with the daring and skill exercised, proves again that crime does not pay—enough.' About like that. Now, can't we get something on a little higher level? We still need three leading articles."

Nat Sperling had no further suggestions to make. I saw it was already 10:45, and with little or nothing done, an early lunch seemed an idle dream. Also, I would have to write off any hope for a conference today with Roy and Hagen. Tony Watson took the ball, speaking in abrupt, nervous rushes and occasionally halting altogether for a moment of pronounced anguish. It seemed to me his neurasthenia could have shown more improvement, if not a complete cure, for the four or five thousand dollars he had spent on psychoanalysis. Still, considering the hazards of our occupation, it could be that without those treatments Tony would today be speechless altogether.

"There's a bulletin by the Welfare Commission," he said, and after we waited for a while he went on, "to be published next month. But we can get copies. I've read it. It's about the criminal abortion racket. Pretty thorough. The commission spent three years investigating. They covered everything, from the small operators to the big, expensive, private s-sanatoriums. Who protects them, why and how. Total estimated number every year, amount of money the industry represents, figures on deaths and prosecutions. Medical effects, pro and con. Causes, results. It's a straight, exhaustive study of the subject. First of its kind. Official, I mean."

Long before Tony had finished, Roy's chin was down upon his chest, and at the close he was making swift notes.

"Do they reach any conclusions? Make any recommendations?" he asked.

"Well, the report gives a complex of causes. Economic reasons are the chief cause of interrupted pregnancies among married women, and among—"

"Never mind that. We'll have to reach our own conclusions. What do they say about old-age assistance?"

"What? Why, nothing, as I recall."

"Never mind, I think we have something. We'll take that bulletin and show what it really means. We'll start by giving the figures for social security survivor benefits. Funeral allowances, in particular, and make the obvious contrasts. Here, on the one hand, is what our government spends every year to bury the dead, while here, at the other end of the scale of life, is what the people spend to prevent birth. Get in touch with the Academy of Medicine and the College of Physicians and Surgeons for a short history of the practice of abortion, and take along a photographer. Maybe they have a collection of primitive and modern in-

[25]

struments. A few pictures ought to be very effective. A short discussion of ancient methods ought to be even more effective."

"Magic was one of them," Bert Finch told Tony.

"Fine," said Roy. "Don't fail to get that in, too. And you might get in touch with the Society of American Morticians for additional figures on what we spend for death, as contrasted with what is spent to prevent life. Call up a half a dozen department stores, ask for figures on what the average expectant mother spends on clothes and equipment up to the date of birth. And don't forget to bring in a good quotation or two from Jonathan Swift on Irish babies."

He looked at Tony, whose meager, freckled features seemed charged with reserve.

"That isn't exactly what I had in mind, Roy. I thought we'd simply dramatize the findings. The commission's findings."

Roy drew a line under the notes on his pad.

"That's what we will be doing, a take-out on the abortion racket. A round-up of the whole subject of inheritance and illegitimacy. But we will be examining it on a higher level, that's all. Just go ahead with the story now, and when the bulletin comes out we'll check through it and draw attention to the real implications of the general picture, at the same time pointing out the survey's omissions. But don't wait for the survey to be released. Can you have a rough draft in, say, two or three weeks?"

Tony Watson's strangled silence indicated that about two thousand dollars' worth of treatments had been shot to hell. Presently, though, he announced: "I can try."

The conference went on, like all those that had gone

before, and, unless some tremendous miracle intervened, like many hundreds sure to follow.

Next month Nat Sperling's quadruple-slaying on a lonely farm would become a penthouse shooting in Chicago, Tony's bent for sociological research would produce new parole-board reports, novel insurance statistics, a far-reaching decision of the Supreme Court. Whatever the subject, it scarcely mattered. What did matter was our private and collective virtuosity.

Down the hall, in Sydney's office, there was a window out of which an almost forgotten associate editor had long ago jumped. I occasionally wondered whether he had done so after some conference such as this. Just picked up his notes and walked down the corridor to his own room, opened the window, and then stepped out.

But we were not insane.

We were not children exchanging solemn fantasies in some progressive nursery. Nor were the things we were doing here completely useless.

What we decided in this room, more than a million of our fellow-citizens would read three months from now, and what they read they would accept as final. They might not know they were doing so, they might even briefly dispute our decisions, but still they would follow the reasoning we presented, remember the phrases, the tone of authority, and in the end their crystallized judgments would be ours.

Where our own logic came from, of course, was still another matter. The moving impulse simply arrived, and we, on the face that the giant clock turned to the public, merely registered the correct hour of the standard time.

But being the measure by which so many lives were shaped and guided gave us, sometimes, strange delusions.

At five minutes to twelve, even the tentative schedule lined up for the April book was far too meager. Leon Temple and Roy were engaged in a rather aimless cross-discussion about a radio program that Leon construed as a profound conspiracy against reason, and therefore a cardinal crime, with Roy protesting the program was only a minor nuisance.

"It's on a pretty low level, and why should we give it free advertising?" he demanded. "Like inferior movies and books and plays, it's simply not on our map."

"And like confidence games, and counterfeit money," Leon jibed.

"I know, Leon, but after all—"

"But after all," I intervened, "it's noon, and we've come around to ultimate values, right on the dot."

Roy looked around, smiling. "Well, if you have something, don't let it spoil."

"I think maybe I have," I said. "A little idea that might do everyone a certain amount of good, ourselves included. It's about *Futureways*. We all know something of what they're doing downstairs."

"Those alchemists," said Roy. "Do they know, themselves?"

"I have a strong feeling they've lost their way with Funded Individuals," I began. "We could do a double service by featuring it ourselves, at the same time sending up a trial balloon for them."

I elaborated. In theory, Funded Individuals was something big. The substance of it was the capitalization of gifted people in their younger years for an amount sufficient to rear them under controlled conditions, educate them, and then provide for a substantial investment in some profitable enterprise through which the original indebtedness would be repaid. The original loan, floated as ordinary stocks or bonds, also paid life-insurance premiums guaranteeing the full amount of the issue, and a normal yearly dividend.

Not every one of these incorporated people—Funded Individuals was our registered name for the undertaking— would be uniformly successful, of course, however fortunate and talented he might originally be. But the Funded Individuals were operated as a pool, with a single directorship, and our figures had demonstrated that such a venture would ultimately show a tremendous overall profit.

It went without saying that the scheme would mean a great deal to those persons chosen for the pool. Each would be capitalized at something like one million dollars, from the age of seventeen.

I told the staff that the social implications of such a project, carried to its logical conclusions, meant the end of not only poverty, ignorance, disease, and maladjustment, but also inevitably of crime.

"We can suggest a new approach to the whole problem of crime," I concluded. "Crime is no more inherent in society than diphtheria, horse-cars, or black magic. We are accustomed to thinking that crime will cease only in some far-off Utopia. But the conditions for abolishing it are at hand—right now."

The idea was tailored for *Crimeways*, and the staff knew it. Roy said, cautiously: "Well, it does show a perspective of diminishing crime." His thin face was filled with a whole train of afterthoughts. "I see where it could be ours. But what about those people downstairs? And what about the thirty-second floor? It's their material, and they have their own ideas about what to do with it, haven't they?"

I said I didn't think so. Mafferson, Orlin, and half a dozen

[29]

others downstairs in the research bureau known as *Future-ways* had been working on Funded Individuals off and on for nearly a year, with no visible results as yet, and with slight probability there ever would be. I said: "The point is, they don't know whether they want to drop Funded Individuals, or what to do with it if they don't. I think Hagen would welcome any sort of a move. We can give the idea an abbreviated prevue."

" 'Crimeless Tomorrow,' " Roy improvised. " 'Research Shows Why. Finance Shows How.' " He thought for a moment. "But I don't see any pictures, George."

"Graphs."

We let it go at that. That afternoon I cleared the article with Hagen, in a three-minute phone call. Then I had a talk with Ed Orlin, who agreed that Emory Mafferson would be the right man to work with us, and presently Emory put in his appearance.

I knew him only casually. He was not much more than five feet high, and gave the illusion he was taller sitting than standing. He radiated a slight, steady aura of confusion.

After we checked over his new assignment he brought forward a personal matter.

"Say, George."

"Yes?"

"How are you fixed on the staff of *Crimeways?* After we line up Funded Individuals?"

"Why, do you want to join us?"

"Well, I damn near have to. Ed Orlin looked almost happy when he found I was being borrowed up here."

"Don't you get along with Ed?"

"We get along all right, sometimes. But I begin to think

he's beginning to think I'm not the *Futureways* type. I know the signs. It's happened before, see."

"You write short stories, don't you?"

Emory appeared to grope for the truth. "Well."

"I understand. It's all right with me, Emory, if you want to come on here. What in hell, by the way, is the *Futureways* type?"

Emory's brown eyes swam around behind thick spectacles like two lost and lonely goldfish. The inner concentration was terrific. "First place, you've got to believe you're shaping something. Destiny, for example. And then you'd better not do anything to attract attention to yourself. It's fatal to come up with a new idea, for instance, and it's also fatal not to have any at all. See what I mean? And above all, it's dangerous to turn in a piece of finished copy. Everything has to be serious, and pending. Understand?"

"No. Just don't try to be the *Crimeways* type, that's all I ask."

We got Emory and Bert Finch teamed for the "Crimeless Tomorrow" feature, and at five o'clock I phoned Georgette to say I'd be home, after all, but Nellie told me Georgette had gone to her sister's in some emergency involving one of Ann's children. She would be home late, might not be home at all. I told Nellie I'd have supper in town.

It was five-thirty when I walked into the Silver Lining, alone. I had a drink and reviewed what I would have said to Roy and Steve Hagen, had they been present to listen. It did not sound as convincing as I had made it sound this morning. Yet there must be a way. I could do something, I had to, and I would.

The bar of the Silver Lining is only twenty feet from the nearest tables. Behind me, at one of them, I heard a woman's voice saying that she really must leave, and then another voice saying they would have to meet again soon. Half turning, I saw the first speaker depart, and then I saw the other woman. It was Pauline Delos. The face, the voice, and the figure registered all at once.

We looked at each other across half the width of the room, and before I had quite placed her I had smiled and nodded. So did she, and in much the same manner.

I picked up my drink and went to her table. Why not?

I said of course she didn't remember me, and she said of course she did.

I said could I buy her a drink. I could.

She was blonde as hell, wearing a lot of black.

"You're the friend of President McKinley," she told me. I admitted it. "And this was where you were talking to him. Is he here tonight?"

I looked all around the room.

I guess she meant Clyde Polhemus, but he wasn't here.

"Not tonight," I said. "How would you like to have dinner with me, instead?"

"I'd love it."

I think we had an apple-brandy sidecar to begin with. It did not seem this was only the second time we had met. All at once a whole lot of things were moving and mixing, as though they had always been there.

GEORGE STROUD IV

WE WERE in the Silver Lining for about an hour. We had dinner there, after Pauline made a phone call rearranging some previous plans.

Then we made the studio broadcast of *Rangers of the Sky;* the program itself was one of my favorites, but that was not the main attraction. We could have heard it anywhere, on any set. Quite aside from the appeal of the program, I was fascinated by the work of a new sound-effects man who, I believed, was laying the foundation for a whole new radio technique. This chap could run a sequence of dramatic sound, without voice or music, for as much as five minutes. Sustaining the suspense, and giving it a clear meaning, too. I explained to Pauline, who seemed puzzled but interested, that some day this fellow would do a whole fifteen- or thirty-minute program of sound and nothing but sound, without voice or music of course, a drama with no words, and then radio would have grown up.

After that Pauline made some more phone calls, rearranging some other plans, and I remembered Gil's bar on Third Avenue. It wasn't exactly a bar and it wasn't exactly a night club; perhaps it might have been called a small Coney Island, or just a dive. Or maybe Gil had the right name and description when he called it a museum.

I hadn't been there for a year or two, but when I had been, there was a game Gil played with his friends and customers, and to me it had always seemed completely worth while.

Although most of Gil's was an ordinary greased postage stamp for dancing to any kind of a band, with any kind of entertainment, there was one thing about it that was different. There was a thirty-foot bar, and on a deep shelf in back of it Gil had accumulated and laid out an inexhaustible quantity of junk—there is no other word for it—which he called his "personal museum." It was Gil's claim that everything in the world was there, somewhere, and that the article, whatever it was, had a history closely connected with his own life and doings. The game was to stump him, on one point or the other.

I never had, though all told I certainly had spent many happy hours trying to do so, and lots of money. At the same time, Gil's logic was sometimes strained and his tales not deeply imaginative. There was a recurrent rumor that every time Gil got stuck for something not in stock, he made it a point to go out and get its equivalent, thus keeping abreast of alert students of the game. Furthermore, his ripostes in the forenoon and early afternoon of the day were not on a par with the results achieved later on, when he was drunk.

"Anything?" Pauline asked, surveying the collection.

"Anything at all," I assured her.

We were seated at the bar, which was not very crowded, and Pauline was looking in mild astonishment at the deceptive forest of bric-a-brac facing us. There was even a regular bar mirror behind all that mountain of gadgets, as I knew from personal experience. Shrunken heads, franc notes, mark notes, confederate money, bayonets, flags, a piece of a totem pole, an airplane propeller, some mounted birds and butterflies, rocks and seashells, surgical instruments, postage stamps, ancient newspapers—wherever the eye wandered it saw some other incongruity and slipped rather dazedly on to still more.

Gil came up, beaming, and I saw he was in form. He knew me by sight only. He nodded, and I said: "Gil, the lady wants to play the game."

"Surely," he said. Gil was an affable fifty, I would have guessed, or maybe fifty-five. "What can I show you, Miss?"

I said, "Can you show us a couple of highballs, while she makes up her mind?"

He took our orders and turned to set them up.

"Anything at all?" Pauline asked me. "No matter how ridiculous?"

"Lady, those are Gil's personal memoirs. You wouldn't call a man's life ridiculous, would you?"

"What did he have to do with the assassination of Abraham Lincoln?"

She was looking at the headline of a yellowed, glass-encased newspaper announcing same. Of course, I had once wondered the same thing, and I told her: The paper was a family heirloom; Gil's grandfather had written the headline, when he worked for Horace Greeley.

"Simple," I pointed out. "And don't ask for lady's hats. He's got Cleopatra's turban back there, and half a dozen other moth-eaten relics that could pass for anything at all."

Gil slid our drinks before us, and gave Pauline his most professional smile.

"I want to see a steamroller," she said.

Gil's beam deepened and he went down the bar, returned with a black and jagged metal cylinder that had once served, if I properly remembered a wild evening, as Christopher Columbus' telescope—a relic certified by the Caribbean natives from whom Gil had personally secured it.

"I can't show you the whole steamroller, ma'am," Gil told Pauline. "Naturally, I haven't room here. Someday I'll have a bigger place, and then I can enlarge my personal museum. But this here is the safety valve from off a steamroller, this is. Go on," he pushed it at her. "It's a very clever arrangement. Look it over."

Pauline accepted the article, without bothering to look at it.

"And this is part of your personal museum?"

"The last time they paved Third Avenue," Gil assured her, "this here steamroller exploded right out in front there. The safety valve, which you have ahold of right there in your hand, came through the window like a bullet. Creased me. As a matter of fact, it left a scar. Look, I'll show you." I knew that scar, and he showed it again. That scar was Gil's biggest asset. "The valve off that steamroller was defective, as you can tell by looking at it. But, as long as it was right here anyway, why, I just left it up in back of the bar where it hit. It was one of the narrowest escapes I ever had."

"Me too," I said. "I was right here when it happened. What'll you have, Gil?"

"Why, I don't mind."

Gil turned and earnestly poured himself a drink, his honest reward for scoring. We lifted our glasses, and Gil jerked his gray, massive head just once. Then he went down the bar to an amateur customer who loudly demanded to see a pink elephant.

Gil patiently showed him the pink elephant, and courteously explained its role in his life.

"I like the museum," said Pauline. "But it must be terrible, sometimes, for Gil. He's seen everything, done everything, gone everywhere, known everyone. What's left for him?"

I muttered that history would be in the making tomorrow, the same as today, and we had another drink on that thought. And then Gil came back and Pauline had another experiment with his memories, and the three of us had another round. And then another.

At one o'clock we were both tired of Gil's life, and I began to think of my own.

I could always create a few more memories, myself. Why not?

There were many reasons why I should not. I weighed them all again, and I tried once more to explain somehow the thing that I knew I was about to do. But they all slipped away from me.

I conjured all sorts of very fancy explanations, besides the simple one, but either the plain or the fancy reasons were good enough; I was not particular on what grounds I behaved foolishly, and even dangerously.

Perhaps I was tired of doing, always, what I ought to do, wearier still of not doing the things that should not be done.

The attractions of the Delos woman multiplied themselves by ten, and then presently they were multiplying by the hundreds. We looked at each other, and that instant was like the white flash of a thrown switch when a new circuit is formed and then the current flows invisibly through another channel.

Why not? I knew the risks and the cost. And still, why not? Maybe the risks and the price were themselves at least some of the reasons why. The cost would be high; it would take some magnificent lying and acting; yet if I were willing to pay that price, why not? And the dangers would be greater still. Of them, I couldn't even begin to guess.

But it would be a very rousing thing to spend an evening with this blonde mystery that certainly ought to be solved. And if I didn't solve it now, I never would. Nobody ever would. It would be something lost forever.

"Well?" she said.

She was smiling, and I realized I had been having an imaginary argument with a shadow of George Stroud standing just in back of the blazing nimbus she had become. It was amazing. All that other Stroud seemed to be saying was: *Why not?* Whatever he meant, I couldn't imagine. Why not what?

I finished a drink I seemed to have in my hand, and said: "I'll have to make a phone call."

"Yes. So will I."

My own phone call was to a nearby semi-residential hotel. The manager had never failed me—I was putting his sons and daughters through school, wasn't I?—and he didn't fail me now. When I returned from the booth, I said: "Shall we go?"

"Let's. Is it far?"

"Not far," I said. "But it's nothing extravagant."

I had no idea, of course, where in that rather sad and partially respectable apartment-hotel we would find ourselves. Pauline took all this for granted, apparently. It gave me a second thought; and the second thought whisked itself away the moment it occurred. Then I hoped she wouldn't say anything about anyone or anything except ourselves.

I needn't have worried. She didn't.

These moments move fast, if they are going to move at

all, and with no superfluous nonsense. If they don't move, they die.

Bert Sanders, the manager of the Lexington-Plaza, handed me a note when he gave me the key to a room on the fifth floor. The note said he positively must have the room by noon tomorrow, reservations had been made for it. The room itself, where I found my in-town valise, was all right, a sizable family vault I believed I had lived in once or twice before.

I was a little bit surprised and dismayed to see it was already three o'clock, as I brought out the half bottle of Scotch, the one dressing gown and single pair of slippers, the back number of *Crimeways*—how did that get here?— the three volumes of stories and poetry, the stack of handkerchiefs, pajamas, aspirin tablets comprising most of the contents of the valise. I said: "How would you like some Scotch?"

We both would. Service in the Lexington-Plaza perished at about ten o'clock, so we had our drinks with straight tap water. It was all right. The life we were now living seemed to quicken perceptibly.

I remembered to tell Pauline, lying on the floor with a pillow under her head and looking more magnificent than ever in my pajamas, that our home would no longer be ours after noon. She dreamily told me I needn't worry, it would be all right, and why didn't I go right on explaining about Louise Patterson and the more important trends in modern painting. I saw with some surprise I had a book open in my lap, but I had been talking about something else entirely. And now I couldn't remember what. I dropped the book, and lay down on the floor beside her.

"No more pictures," I said. "Let's solve the mystery."

"What mystery?"

"You."

"I'm a very average person, George. No riddle at all."

I believe I said, "You're the last, final, beautiful, beautiful, ultimate enigma. Maybe you can't be solved."

And I think I looked at our great big gorgeous bed, soft and deep and wide. But it seemed a thousand miles away. I decided it was just too far. But that was all right. It was better than all right. It was perfect. It was just plain perfect.

I found out again why we are on this earth. I think.

And then I woke up and saw myself in that big, wide bed, alone, with a great ringing and hammering and buzzing going on. The phone was closest, so I answered it, and a voice said: "I'm sorry, sir, but Mr. Sanders says you have no reservation for today."

I looked at my watch; 1:30.

"All right."

I believe I moaned and lay back and ate an aspirin tablet that somebody had thoughtfully laid on the table beside the bed, and then after a while I went to the door that was still pounding and buzzing. It was Bert Sanders.

"You all right?" he asked, looking more than a little worried. "You know, I told you I've reserved this suite."

"My God."

"Well, I hate to wake you up, but we have to—"

"All right."

"I don't know exactly when—"

"My God."

"If I'd thought—"

"All right. Where is she?"

"Who? Oh, well, about six o'clock this morning—"

"My God, never mind."

"I thought you'd want to sleep for a few hours, but—"

"All right." I found my trousers and my wallet and I somehow paid off Bert. "I'll be out of here in three minutes. Was there anything, by the way—?"

"Nothing, Mr. Stroud. It's just that this room—"

"Sure. Get my bag out of here, will you?"

He said he would, and after that I got dressed in a hurry, looking around the room for possible notes as I found a clean shirt, washed but did not attempt to shave, poured myself a fraction of an inch that seemed to be left in a bottle of Scotch somehow on hand.

Who was she?

Pauline Delos. Janoth's girl friend. Oh, God. What next?

Where did Georgette think I was? In town, on a job, but coming home a little late. All right. And then?

What was I supposed to be doing at the office today?

I couldn't remember anything important, and that was not so bad.

But about the major problems? Well, there was nothing I could do about them now, if I had been as stupid as all this. Nothing. Well, all right.

I combed my hair, brushed my teeth, put on my tie.

I could tell Georgette, at her sister's in Trenton, that I had to work until three in the morning and didn't want to phone. It would have awakened the whole household. Simple. It had always worked before. It would work this time. Had to.

I closed my valise, left it for Bert in the middle of the room, went downstairs to the barber shop in the lobby. There I got a quick shave, and after that I had a quicker breakfast, and then a split-second drink.

It was three o'clock in the afternoon when I got back to my desk, and there was no one around except Lucille, Roy's and my secretary, listlessly typing in the small room connecting our two offices. She did not appear curious, and I couldn't find any messages on my desk, either, just a lot of inter-office memos and names.

"Anyone phone me, Lucille?" I asked.

"Just those on your pad."

"My home didn't call? Nothing from my wife?"

"No."

So it was all right. So far. Thank God.

I went back to my desk and sat down and took three more aspirin tablets. It was an afternoon like any other afternoon, except for those nerves. But there should be nothing really the matter with them, either. I began to go through the routine items listed by Lucille. Everything was the same as it had always been. Everything was all right. I hadn't done anything. No one had.

GEORGE STROUD V

AND ALL of that went off all right. And
two months passed. And during those
two months, Mafferson and I worked up the data and the
groundwork for Funded Individuals, and we also worked
up a take-out of bankruptcy for the May issue, and a de-
tailed story about bought-and-sold orphans for the June
book.

Then one evening, early in March, I had one of those
moods. I reached for the phone, and from our confidential
telephone service got the number I wanted. When the number answered I said: "Hello, Pauline. This is your attorney."

"Oh, yes," she said, after a second. "That one."

It was a spring day, I told her, as it was: the first. We
fixed it to have cocktails at the Van Barth.

Georgette and Georgia were in Florida, returning in
two days. Earl Janoth was in Washington, for at least a
couple of hours, and possibly for a week. It was a Friday.

Before leaving that night I stepped into Roy's office and
found him conferring with Emory Mafferson and Bert
Finch. I gathered that Emory was filled with doubts regarding "Crimeless Tomorrow, Science Shows Why, Finance Shows How."

Emory said: "I can see, on paper, how Funded Individuals works out fine. I can see from the insurance rates
and the business statistics that it works out for a few people who happen to be funded, but what I don't see is, what's

going to happen if everyone belongs to the corporation pool? See what I'm driving at?"

Roy was being at his confident, patient, understanding best. "That's what it's supposed to lead to," he said. "And I think it's rather nice. Don't you?"

"Let me put it this way, Roy. If a person capitalized at a million dollars actually returns the original investment, plus a profit, then there's going to be a tremendous rush to incorporate still more individuals, for still more profit. And pretty soon, everyone will be in clover except the stockholders. What do they get out of the arrangement?"

Roy's patience took on palpable weight and shape. "Profit," he said.

"Sure, but what can they do with it? What have they got? Just some monetary gain. They don't, themselves, lead perfectly conditioned lives, with a big sum left over to invest in some new, paying enterprise. Seems to me the only people that get it in the neck with this scheme are the subscribers who make the whole thing possible."

Roy said: "You forget that after this has been in operation a few years, funded people will themselves be the first to reinvest their capital in the original pool, so that both groups are always interested parties of the same process."

I decided they were doing well enough without interference from me, and left.

In the bar of the Van Barth I met a beautiful stranger in a rather austere gray and black ensemble that looked like a tailored suit, but wasn't. I hadn't been waiting for more than ten minutes. After we settled on the drink she would have, Pauline said, rather seriously: "I shouldn't be here at all, you know. I have a feeling it's dangerous to know you."

"Me? Dangerous? Kittens a month old get belligerent when they see me coming. Open their eyes for the first time and sharpen up their claws, meowing in anticipation."

She smiled, without humor, and soberly repeated: "You're a dangerous person, George."

I didn't think this was the right note to strike, and so I struck another one. And pretty soon it was all right, and we had another drink, and then after a while we went to Lemoyne's for supper.

I had been living pretty much alone for the last three weeks, since Georgette and Georgia had gone to Florida, and I felt talkative. So I talked. I told her the one about what the whale said to the submarine, why the silents had been the Golden Age of the movies, why Lonny Trout was a fighter's fighter, and then I suggested that we drive up to Albany.

That is what we finally did. I experienced again the pleasure of driving up the heights of the only perfect river in the world, the river that never floods, never dries up, and yet never seems to be the same twice. Albany we reached, by stages, in about three hours.

I had always liked the city, too, which is not as commonplace as it may look to the casual traveler, particularly when the legislature is in session. If there is anything Manhattan has overlooked, it settled here.

After registering under a name I dreamed up with some care and imagination, Mr. and Mrs. Andrew Phelps-Guyon, we went out and spent a couple of hours over food and drink, some entertainment and a few dances on a good, not crowded floor, at a damnably expensive night club. But it was an evening with a definite touch of spring, snatched from the very teeth of the inner works, and exceedingly worth while.

[45]

We had breakfast at about noon, and shortly afterwards started a slow drive back to the city, by a different route. It was a different river we followed again, of course, and of course, I fell in love with it all over again; and of course, Pauline helped.

It was late Saturday afternoon when we reached the neighborhood of 58 East, Pauline's apartment building, so early she admitted she had time and lots of it. We went to Gil's. Pauline played the game for about three rounds. I thought Gil was stuck when she asked to see Poe's Raven, but he brought out a stuffed bluebird or something, well advanced in its last molting, and explained it was Poe's original inspiration, personally presented to his close friend, Gil's great-grandfather. And then I remembered it was a long time, all of three months, since I'd explored Antique Row.

That is Third Avenue from about Sixtieth Street all the way down to Forty-second, or thereabouts; there may be bigger, better, more expensive and more authentic shops scattered elsewhere about the city, but the spirit of adventure and rediscovery is not in them, somehow. I once asked, on a tall evening in a Third Avenue shop, for the Pied Piper of Hamlin's pipe. They happened to have it, too. I forget what I did with it, after I bought it for about ten dollars and took it first to the office, where it seemed to have lost its potency, and then home, where somebody broke it and then it disappeared. But it wasn't Third Avenue's fault if I hadn't known how to take care of it properly.

This afternoon Pauline and I dawdled over some not very interesting early New England bedwarmers, spinning wheels converted to floor and table lamps, and the usual commodes disguised as playchairs, bookshelves, and tea carts. All very sound and substantial stuff, reflecting more credit to the ingenuity of the twentieth century than to the imagination of the original craftsmen. It was interesting, some of it, but not exciting.

Then at about half-past seven, with some of the shops closing, we reached a little but simply jam-packed place on Fiftieth Street. Maybe I had been in here before, but I couldn't remember it and neither, seemingly, did the proprietor remember me.

I rummaged about for several minutes without his help, not seeing anything I may have missed before, but I had a fine time answering Pauline's questions. Then after a while somebody else came in and I became increasingly aware of the dialogue going forward at the front of the shop.

"Yes, I have," I heard the dealer say, with some surprise. "But I don't know if they're exactly the type you'd want. Hardly anyone asks for pictures in here, of course. I just put that picture in the window because it happened to be framed. Is that the one you wanted?"

"No. But you have some others, haven't you? Unframed. A friend of mine was in here a couple of weeks ago and said you had."

The customer was a big, monolithic brunette, sloppily dressed and with a face like an arrested cyclone.

"Yes, I have. They're not exactly in perfect condition."

"I don't care," she said. "May I see them?"

The dealer located a roll of canvases on an overhead shelf, and tugged them down. I had drifted down to the front of the shop by now, constituting myself a silent partner in the proceedings. The dealer handed the woman the entire roll, and I practically rested my chin on his left shoulder.

"Look them over," he told the woman.

He turned his head, frowning, and for a fraction of a moment one of his eyes loomed enormously, gazing into one of mine. Mine expressed polite curiosity.

"Where did you get these?" the customer asked.

She unrolled the sheaf of canvases, which were about four by five, some more and some less, and studied the one on top from her reverse viewpoint. It showed a Gloucester clipper under full sail, and it was just like all pictures of clippers, unusual only for a ring of dirt, like an enlarged coffee ring, that wreathed the vessel and several miles of the ocean. To say it was not exactly in perfect condition was plain perjury. The ring, I thought, was about the size of a barrelhead, and that would be about where it came from.

"They were part of a lot," the dealer guardedly told her. The big woman cut loose with a loud, ragged laugh. "Part of a lot of what?" she asked. "Material for an arson? Or is this some of that old WPA stuff they used to wrap up ten-cent store crockery?"

"I don't know where it came from. I told you it wasn't in the best of shape."

She thrust the one on top to the rear, exposing a large bowl of daisies. Nobody said anything at all, this time; I just closed my eyes for a couple of seconds and it went away.

The third canvas was an honest piece of work of the tenement-and-junkyard school; I placed it as of about fifteen years ago; I didn't recognize the signature, but it could have been painted by one of five or six hundred good, professional artists who had done the same scene a little better or a little worse.

"Pretty good," said the shop proprietor. "Colorful. It's real."

The tall, square brunette intently went on to the next one. It was another Gloucester clipper, this one going the other way. It had the same magnificent coffee ring that they all did. And the next one was a basket of kittens. "My Pets," I am sure the nice old lady who painted it had called this one. Anyway, the show was diversified. Clipper artists stuck to clippers, backyard painters did them by the miles, and the nice old lady had certainly done simply hundreds and hundreds of cats. Our gallery had them all.

"I'm afraid you haven't got anything here that would interest me," said the woman.

The man tacitly admitted it, and she resumed the show. Two more pictures passed without comment, and I saw there were only two or three more.

Then she turned up another one, methodically, and I suddenly stopped breathing. It was a Louise Patterson. There was no mistaking the subject, the treatment, the effect. The brothers and sisters of that picture hung on my walls in Marble Road. I had once paid nine hundred dollars for one of them, not much less for the others, all of which I had picked up at regular Patterson shows on Fifty-seventh Street.

The customer had already slipped a tentative finger in back of it to separate it from the next canvas and take it away, when I cleared my throat and casually remarked: "I rather like that."

She looked at me, not very amiably, swung the picture around and held it up before her, at arm's length; it curled at the edges where it wasn't frayed, and it had a few spots of something on it in addition to the trademark of the outsized coffee ring. It was in a frightful condition, no less.

"So do I," she flatly declared. "But it's in one hell of a shape. How much do you want for it?"

The question, ignoring me entirely, was fired at the dealer.

"Why—"

"God, what a mess."

With her second shot she doubtless cut the dealer's intended price in half.

"I wouldn't know how to value it, exactly," he admitted. "But you can have it for ten dollars?"

It was the literal truth that I did not myself know what a Patterson would be worth, today, on the regular market. Nothing fabulous, I knew; but on the other hand, although Patterson hadn't exhibited for years, and for all I knew was dead, it did not seem possible her work had passed into complete eclipse. The things I had picked up for a few hundred had been bargains when I bought them, and later still the artist's canvases had brought much more, though only for a time.

I beamed at the woman. "I spoke first," I said to her, and then to the dealer: "I'll give you fifty for it."

The dealer, who should have stuck to refinished porch furniture, was clearly dazzled and also puzzled. I could tell the exact moment the great electric light went on in his soul: he had something, probably a Rembrandt.

"Well, I don't know," he said. "It's obviously a clever picture. Extremely sound. I was intending to have this lot appraised, when I had the time. This is the first time I've really looked at the lot, myself. I think—"

"It is not a Raphael, Rubens, or Corot," I assured him.

He leaned forward and looked more closely at the picture. The canvas showed two hands, one giving and the other receiving a coin. That was all. It conveyed the whole feeling, meaning, and drama of money. But the proprietor was unwrinkling the bottom right-hand corner of the canvas, where the signature would be rather legibly scrawled. I began to perspire.

"Pat something," he announced, studying it carefully, and the next moment he sounded disappointed. "Oh. Patterson, '32. I ought to know that name, but it's slipped my mind."

I let this transparent perjury die a natural death. The large brunette, built like an old-fashioned kitchen cabinet, didn't say anything either. But she didn't need to. She obviously didn't have fifty dollars. And I had to have that picture.

"It's a very superior work," the dealer began again. "When it's cleaned up, it'll be beautiful."

"I like it," I said. "For fifty bucks."

He said, stalling: "I imagine the fellow who painted it called the picture *Toil*. Something like that."

"I'd call it *Judas*," Pauline spoke up. "No, *The Temptation of Judas*."

"There's only one coin," said the dealer, seriously. "There would have to be thirty." Still stalling, he took the canvases and began to go through those we had not seen. A silo, with a cow in front of it. A nice thing with some children playing in the street. The beach at Coney Island. Depressed at stirring no further interest, he declared, "And that's all I have."

To the brunette, and smiling glassily, I said: "Why don't you take the *Grand Street Children*, for about five dollars? I'll take the *Judas*."

She unchained a whoop of laughter that was not, as far as I could make out, either friendly or hostile. It was just loud.

"No, thanks, I have enough children of my own."

"I'll buy you a frame, we'll fix it here, and you can take it home."

This produced another shriek, followed by a roar.

"Save it for your fifty-dollar masterpiece." This sounded derisive. I asked her, with a bite in it: "Don't you believe it's worth that?"

"A picture that is worth anything at all is certainly worth a lot more than that," she suddenly blazed. "Don't you think so? It is either worth ten dollars or a million times that much." Mentally I agreed with this perfectly reasonable attitude, but the shop proprietor looked as though he did, too. And I had to have that picture. It wasn't my fault I had only sixty odd dollars left after one of the most expensive week ends in history, instead of ten million. "But what do I know about paintings? Nothing. Don't let me interfere. Maybe sometime," there was another blood-curdling laugh, "I'll have the right kind of wallpaper, and just the right space to match the *Grand Street Children*. Save it for me."

She went away, then, and in the quiet that came back to the little shop I firmly proved I would pay what I said I would and no more, and eventually we went away, too, and I had my prize.

Pauline still had some time, and we stopped in at the cocktail lounge of the Van Barth. I left the canvas in the car, but when we'd ordered our drinks Pauline asked me why on earth I'd bought it, and I described it again, trying to explain. She finally said she liked it well enough, but could not see there was anything extraordinarily powerful about it.

It became evident she was picture-blind. It wasn't her fault; many people are born that way; it is the same as being color-blind or tone-deaf. But I tried to explain what the work of Louise Patterson meant in terms of simplified abstractionism and fresh intensifications of color. Then I argued that the picture must have some feeling for her since she'd surely picked the right title for it.

"How do you know it's right?" she asked.

"I know it. I feel it. It's just what I saw in the picture myself."

On the spur of the moment I decided, and told her, that Judas must have been a born conformist, a naturally common-sense, rubber-stamp sort of fellow who rose far above himself when he became involved with a group of people who were hardly in society, let alone a profitable business.

"Heavens, you make him sound like a saint," Pauline said, smiling and frowning.

I told her very likely he was.

"A man like that, built to fall into line but finding himself always out of step, must have suffered twice the torments of the others. And eventually, the temptation was too much for him. Like many another saint, when he was tempted, he fell. But only briefly."

"Isn't that a little involved?"

"Anyway, it's the name of my picture," I said. "Thanks for your help."

We drank to that, but Pauline upset her cocktail.

I rescued her with my handkerchief for a hectic moment, then left her to finish the job while I called the waiter for more drinks, and he cleared the wet tabletop. After a while we had something to eat, and still more drinks, and a lot more talk.

It was quite dark when we came out of the lounge, and I drove the few blocks to 58 East. Pauline's apartment, which I had never been in, was in one of those austere and permanent pueblos of the Sixties. She asked me to stop away from the entrance, cool as she explained: "I don't think it would be wise for me to go in with a strange overnight bag. Accompanied."

The remark didn't say anything, but it gave me a momentarily uncomfortable measure of the small but nevertheless real risks we were running. I erased that idea and said nothing, but I ran past the building and parked half a block from the lighted, canopied entrance.

There I got out to hand her the light valise she had brought with her to Albany, and for a moment we paused.

"May I phone?" I asked.

"Of course. Please do. But we have to be—well—"

"Of course. It's been wonderful, Pauline. Just about altogether supreme."

She smiled and turned away.

Looking beyond her retreating shoulders I vaguely noticed a limousine pull in at the curb opposite the building's entrance. There was something familiar about the figure and carriage of the man who got out of it. He put his head back into the car to issue instructions to a chauffeur, then turned for a moment in my direction. I saw that it was Earl Janoth.

He noticed Pauline approaching, and I am certain that he looked past her and saw me. But I did not think he could have recognized me; the nearest street lamp was at my back.

And what if he had? He didn't own the woman.

He didn't own me, either.

I stepped into my car and started the motor, and I saw them disappearing together into the lighted entrance.

I didn't feel very happy about this unlucky circumstance, as I drove off, but on the other hand, I didn't see how any irreparable damage could have been done.

I drove back to Gil's. There, it was the usual raucous Saturday night. I had a whole lot of drinks, without much conversation, then I took the car around to my garage and caught the 1:45 for home. It was early, but I wanted to be clear-eyed when Georgette and Georgia got back from Florida in the afternoon. I would return by train, pick them up in the car, and drive them home.

I brought in my own bag, at Marble Road, and of course I didn't forget *The Temptation of St. Judas.* The picture I simply laid down on the dining room table. It would have to be cleaned, repaired, and framed.

I glanced at the Pattersons in the downstairs rooms and at the one upstairs in my study, before I went to bed. The *Temptation* was better than any of them.

It occurred to me that maybe I was becoming one of the outstanding Patterson collectors in the United States. Or anywhere.

But before I went to bed I unpacked my grip, put away the belongings it had contained, then put the grip away, too.

EARL JANOTH I

BY GOD, I never had such an evening. I flatter myself that I am never inurbane by impulse only, but these people, supposedly friends of mine, were the limit, and I could have strangled them one by one.

Ralph Beeman, my attorney for fifteen years, showed damned little interest and less sympathy when the question of the wire renewal for *Commerce Index* came up, or was deliberately brought up. The whole bunch of them quite openly discussed the matter, as though I myself were some sort of immaterial pneuma, not quite present at all, and as though I might actually lose the franchise. Really, they weighed alternatives, when I did lose it.

"Ralph and I have something to say about that," I said, heartily, but the mousey bastard didn't turn a hair. He was just plain neutral.

"Oh, certainly. We'll renew no matter whom we have to fight."

To me, it sounded as though he thought the fight was already lost. I gave him a sharp look, but he chose not to understand. It would have been well, had Steve been present. He is immensely alert to such winds and undercurrents as I felt, but could not measure, everywhere around me.

Ten of us were having dinner at John Wayne's, and since he is a smooth but capable political leader, if we were discussing anything at all it should have been politics. But by God, since I came into his home, a festering old incubus dating back at least a hundred years, we hadn't talked about anything except Janoth Enterprises, and what difficulties we were having. But I wasn't having any difficulties. And I wasn't having any of this, either.

Then there was an awkward moment when Hamilton Carr asked me how I had made out in Washington. I had just returned, and I had an uncomfortable feeling that he knew exactly everyone I had seen there and what I was about. Yet it was really nothing. I had thought of broadening the corporate basis of Janoth Enterprises, and my trip to Washington was simply to obtain quick and reliable information on what procedure I might follow to achieve that end and fully observe all SEC regulations.

Ralph Beeman had gone down with me, had not said much while we were there, and I gave him another emphatic thought. But it couldn't be. Or were they all, in fact, in some kind of a conspiracy against me? Voyagers to new continents of reason have been caught offguard before.

But Hamilton Carr was no enemy; at least, I had never thought he was; he was simply my banking adviser. He had always known, to the last dime, what the paper issued by Janoth Enterprises was worth, and who held it. Tonight, he said: "You know, Jennett-Donohue still want either to buy or merge."

I gave him a huge laugh.

"Yes," I said. "So do I. What will they sell for?"

Carr smiled; it was icy dissent. God damn you, I thought, what's up?

There was a blasted foreign person present with a fearful English accent who went by the name of Lady Pearsall, or something equally insignificant, and she told me at great length what was wrong with my magazines. Everything was wrong with them, according to her. But it hadn't crossed her mind that I had gone far out of my way to obtain the very best writers and editors, the broadest and richest minds to be had. I had combed the newspapers, the magazines, the finest universities, and paid the highest salaries in the field, to hire what I knew were the finest bunch of journalists ever gathered together under one roof. She gobbled away extensively, her Adam's apple moving exactly like a scrawny turkey's, but to hear her tell it, I had found my writers in the hospitals, insane asylums, and penitentiaries.

I could smile at everything she had to say, but I didn't feel like smiling at what Carr and Beeman and finally a man by the name of Samuel Lydon had to say.

"You know," he told me, "there may not always be the same demand for superior presentation there has been in the past. I've been getting reports from the distributors." Anyone could. It was public knowledge. "I think you would like me to be quite candid with you, Mr. Janoth."

"Certainly."

"Well, the returns on some of your key magazines have shown strange fluctuations. Out of proportion to those of other publications, I mean." I placed him now. He was executive vice-president of a local distributing organization. "I wondered if there was any definitely known reason?"

This was either colossal ignorance or outrageous effrontery. *If I knew of definite reasons.* I looked at him, but didn't bother to reply.

"Maybe it's that astrology magazine of yours," said Geoffrey Balack, ineffectual, vicious, crude, and thoroughly counterfeit. He was some kind of a columnist. I had hired him once, but his work had not seemed too satisfactory, and when he left to take another job I had thought it was a fortunate change all round. Looking at him now, I couldn't remember whether he'd quit, or whether Steve had fired him. Or possibly I had. Offensively, now, he brushed a hand back over the rather thin hair on his head. "That's one I never understood at all. Why?"

I was still smiling, but it cost me an effort.

"I bought that little book, *Stars*, for its title alone. Today it has nothing to do with astrology. It is almost the sole authority in astrophysics."

"Popular?"

That didn't deserve a reply, either. This was what we had once considered a writer with insight and integrity. And good writers cost money, which I was more than glad to pay.

But they were growing more expensive all the time. Other publishing organizations, even though they were not in the same field at all, were always happy to raid our staff, though they rarely tampered with each others'. The advertising agencies, the motion pictures, radio, we were always losing our really good men elsewhere, at prices that were simply fantastic. A man we had found ourselves, and nursed along until we found just the right way to bring out the best and soundest that was in him, might then casually leave us to write trash for some perfume program, or speeches for a political amplifier. Contract or no contract, and at a figure it would be almost ruinous to the rest of the organization if we thought of meeting it.

Either that or they wanted to write books. Or went crazy. Although, God knows, most of them were born that way, and their association with us merely slowed up and postponed the inevitable process for a time.

Well. We still had the finest writers to be had, and the competition only kept us on our toes.

When it came to the point where Jennett-Donohue or Devers & Blair offered twenty-five thousand for a fifteen-thousand-dollar editor, we would go thirty thousand. If radio offered fifty thousand for a man we really had to keep, we'd go to sixty. And when Hollywood began raiding our copy boys and legmen for a million—well, all right. No use being morbid. But sometimes it's impossible not to be.

It was ten o'clock—the earliest moment possible—before I was able to leave. I had enough to worry about, without taking on any extra nonsense from this particular crowd.

It is all a matter of one's inherited nerves and glands. No matter how much one rationalizes, one has either a joyless, negative attitude toward everyone and everything, like these people, and it is purely a matter of the way in which the glands function, or one has a positive and constructive attitude. It is no great credit to me. But neither is it any credit to them.

In the car, I told Bill to drive me home, but halfway there I changed my mind. I told him to drive to Pauline's. Hell, she might even be there. Home was no place to go after an evening squandered among a bunch of imitation cynics, disappointed sentimentalists, and frustrated conspirators.

Without a word Bill spun the wheel and we turned the corner. It reminded me of the way he had always taken my orders, thirty years ago during the hottest part of a circulation war out West, then in the printer's strike upstate. That was why he was with me now. If he wouldn't talk even to me, after thirty odd years, he would never talk to anyone.

When we drew up in front of the place and I got out, I put my head in the window next to him and said: "Go on home, Bill. I'll take a taxi. I don't think I'll need you until tomorrow evening."

He looked at me but said nothing, and eased the car away from the curb.

EARL JANOTH II

O N THE sidewalk I turned to go in, but as I turned, I caught sight of Pauline. She was leaving someone at the next corner. I couldn't see her face, but I recognized her profile, the way she stood and carried herself, and I recognized the hat she had recently helped to design, and the beige coat. As I stood there she started to walk toward me. The man with her I did not recognize at all, though I stared until he turned and stepped into a car, his face still in the shadows.

When Pauline reached me she was smiling and serene, a little warm and a little remote, deliberate as always. I said: "Hello, dear. This is fortunate."

She brushed away an invisible strand of hair, stopped beside me.

"I expected you'd be back yesterday," she said. "Did you have a nice trip, Earl?"

"Fine. Have a pleasant week end?"

"Marvelous. I went riding, swimming, read a grand book, and met some of the most interesting brand-new people."

We had moved into the building by now. I glanced down and saw that she carried an overnight bag.

I could hear though not see somebody moving behind the high screen that partitioned off the apartment switchboard and, as usual, there was no sign of anyone else. Perhaps this isolation was one of the reasons she had liked such a place in the beginning.

There was an automatic elevator, and now it was on the main floor. As I opened the door, then followed her in and pushed the button for five, I nodded toward the street.

"Was he one of them?"

"One of who? Oh, you mean the brand-new people. Yes."

The elevator stopped at five. The inner door slid noise-lessly open, and Pauline herself pushed open the outer door. I followed her the dozen or so carpeted steps to 5 A. Inside the small four-room apartment there was such silence and so much dead air it did not seem it could have been entered for days.

"What were you doing?" I asked.

"Well, first we went to a terrible place on Third Avenue by the name of Gil's. You'd love it. Personally, I thought it was a bore. But it's some kind of a combination between an old archeology foundation, and a saloon. The weirdest mixture. Then after that we went up and down the street shopping for antiques."

"What kind of antiques?"

"Any kind that we thought might be interesting. Finally, we bought a picture, that is, he did, in a shop about three blocks from here. An awful old thing that just came out of a dust-bin. it looked like, and he practically kidnapped it from another customer, some woman who bid for it, too. Nothing but a couple of hands, by an artist named Patterson."

"A couple of what?"

"Hands, darling. Just hands. It was a picture about Judas, as I understand it. Then after that we went to the Van Barth and had a few drinks, and he brought me home. That's where you came in. Satisfied?"

I watched her open the door of the small closet in the lobby and drop her bag inside of it, then close the door and turn to me again with her shining hair, deep eyes, and perfect, renaissance face.

"Sounds like an interesting afternoon," I said. "Who was this brand-new person?"

"Oh. Just a man. You don't know him. His name is George Chester, in advertising."

Maybe. And my name is George Agropolus. But I'd been around a lot longer than she had, or, for that matter, than her boy friend. I looked at her for a moment, without speaking, and she returned the look, a little too intently. I almost felt sorry for the new satellite she'd just left, whoever he was.

She poured us some brandy from a decanter beside the lounge, and across the top of her glass she crinkled her eyes in the intimate way supposed to fit the texture of any moment. I sipped my own, knowing again that everything in the world was ashes. Cold, and spent, and not quite worth the effort. It was a mood that Steve never had, a mood peculiarly my own. The question crossed my mind whether possibly others, too, experienced the same feeling, at least occasionally, but that could hardly be. I said: "At least, this time it's a man."

Sharply, she said: "Just what do you mean by that?"

"You know what I mean."

"Are you bringing up that thing again? Throwing Alice in my face?" Her voice had the sound of a wasp. Avenue Z was never far beneath the surface, with Pauline. "You never forget Alice, do you?"

I finished the brandy and reached for the decanter, poured myself another drink. Speaking with deliberate slowness, and politely, I said: "No. Do you?"

"Why, you goddamn imitation Napoleon, what in hell do you mean?"

I finished the brandy in one satisfying swallow.

"And you don't forget Joanna, do you?" I said, softly. "And that Berleth woman, and Jane, and that female refugee from Austria. And God knows who else. You can't forget any of them, can you, including the next one."

She seemed to choke, for a speechless moment, then she moved like a springing animal. Something, I believe it was an ashtray, went past my head and smashed against the wall, showering me with fine glass.

"You son of a bitch," she exploded. "You talk. You, of all people. *You*. That's priceless."

Mechanically, I reached for the decanter, splashed brandy into my glass. I fumbled for the stopper, trying to replace it. But I couldn't seem to connect.

"Yes?" I said.

She was on her feet, on the other side of the low table, her face a tangle of rage.

"What about you and Steve Hagen?"

I forgot about the stopper, and simply stared.

"What? What about me? And Steve?"

"Do you think I'm blind? Did I ever see you two together when you weren't camping?"

I felt sick and stunned, with something big and black gathering inside of me. Mechanically, I echoed her: "Camping? With Steve?"

"As if you weren't married to that guy, all your life. And as if I didn't know. Go on, you son of a bitch, try to act surprised."

It wasn't me, any more. It was some giant a hundred feet tall, moving me around, manipulating my hands and arms and even my voice. He straightened my legs, and I found myself standing. I could hardly speak. My voice was a sawtoothed whisper.

[65]

"You say this about Steve? The finest man that ever lived? And me?"

"Why, you poor, old carbon copy of that fairy gorilla. Are you so dumb you've lived this long without even knowing it?" Then she suddenly screamed: "Don't. Earl, don't."

I hit her over the head with the decanter and she stumbled back across the room. My voice said: "You can't talk like that. Not about us."

"Don't. Oh, God, Earl, don't. Earl. Earl. Earl."

I had kicked over the table between us, and I moved after her. I hit her again, and she kept talking with that awful voice of hers, and then I hit her twice more.

Then she was lying on the floor, quiet and a little twisted. I said: "There's a limit to this. A man can take just so much."

She didn't reply. She didn't move.

I stood above her for a long, long time. There was no sound at all, except the remote, muffled hum of traffic from the street below. The decanter was still in my hand, and I lifted it, looked at the bottom edge of it faintly smeared, and with a few strands of hair.

"Pauline."

She lay on her back, watching something far away that didn't move. She was pretending to be unconscious.

A fear struck deeper and deeper and deeper, as I stared at her beautiful, bright, slowly bleeding head. Her face had an expression like nothing on earth.

"Oh, God, Pauline. Get up."

I dropped the decanter and placed my hand inside her blouse, over the heart. Nothing. Her face did not change. There was no breath, no pulse, nothing. Only her warmth and faint perfume. I slowly stood up. She was gone.

[66]

So all of my life had led to this strange dream.

A darkness and a nausea flooded in upon me, in waves I had never known before. This, this carrion by-product had suddenly become the total of everything. Of everything there had been between us. Of everything I had ever done. This accident.

For it was an accident. God knows. A mad one.

I saw there were stains on my hands, and my shirt front. There were splotches on my trousers, my shoes, and as my eyes roved around the room I saw that there were even spots high on the wall near the lounge where I had first been sitting.

I needed something. Badly. Help and advice.

I moved into the bathroom and washed my hands, sponged my shirt. It came to me that I must be careful. Careful of everything. I closed the taps with my handkerchief. If her boy friend had been here, and left his own fingerprints. If others had. Anyone else. And many others had.

Back in the other room, where Pauline still lay on the carpet, unchanging, I remembered the decanter and the stopper to it. These I both wiped carefully, and the glass. Then I reached for the phone, and at the same time remembered the switchboard downstairs, and drew away.

I let myself out of the apartment, again using my handkerchief as a glove. Pauline had let us in. The final image of her own fingers would be on the knob, the key, the frame.

I listened for a long moment outside the door of 5A. There was no sound throughout the halls, and none from behind that closed door. I knew, with a renewed vertigo of grief and dread, there would never again be life within that apartment. Not for me.

Yet there had been, once, lots of it. All collapsed to the size of a few single moments that were now a deadly, unreal threat.

I moved quietly down the carpeted hall, and down the stairs. From the top of the first floor landing I could just see the partly bald, gray head of the man at the switchboard. He hadn't moved, and if he behaved as usual, he wouldn't.

I went quietly down the last flight of stairs and moved across the lobby carpet to the door. At the door, when I opened it, I looked back. No one was watching, there was no one in sight.

On the street, I walked for several blocks, then at a stand on some corner I took a taxi. I gave the driver an address two blocks from the address I automatically knew I wanted. It was about a mile uptown.

When I got out and presently reached the building it was as quiet as it had been at Pauline's.

There was no automatic elevator, as there was at Pauline's, and I did not want to be seen, not in this condition. I walked up the four flights to the apartment. I rang, suddenly sure there would be no answer.

But there was.

Steve's kindly, wise, compact, slightly leathery face confronted me when the door swung open. He was in slippers and a dressing gown. When he saw me, he held the door wider, and I came in.

He said: "You look like hell. What is it?"

I walked past him and into his living room and sat down in a wide chair.

"I have no right to come here. But I didn't know where else to go."

[68]

He had followed me into his living room, and he asked, impassively: "What's the matter?"

"God. I don't know. Give me a drink."

Steve gave me a drink. When he said he would ring for some ice, I stopped him.

"Don't bring anyone else in on this," I said. "I've just killed someone."

"Yes?" He waited. "Who?"

"Pauline."

Steve looked at me hard, poured himself a drink, briefly sipped it, still watching me.

"Are you sure?"

This was insane. I suppressed a wild laugh. Instead, I told him, curtly: "I'm sure."

"All right," he said, slowly. "She had it coming to her. You should have killed her three years ago."

I gave him the longest look and the most thought I had ever given him. There was an edge of iron amusement in his locked face. I knew what was going on in his mind: *She was a tramp, why did you bother with her?* And I know what went on in my mind: *I am about the loneliest person in the world.*

"I came here, Steve," I said, "because this is just about my last stop. I face, well, everything. But I thought—hell, I don't know what I thought. But if there is anything I should do, well. I thought maybe you'd know what that would be."

"She deserved it," Steve quietly repeated. "She was a regular little comic."

"Steve, don't talk like that about Pauline. One of the warmest, most generous women who ever lived."

He finished his drink and casually put down the glass.

"Was she? Why did you kill her?"

"I don't know, I just don't know. From here I go to Ralph Beeman, and then to the cops, and then I guess to prison or even the chair." I finished my drink and put down the glass. "I'm sorry I disturbed you."

Steve gestured. "Don't be a fool," he said. "Forget that prison stuff. What about the organization? Do you know what will happen to it the second you get into serious trouble?"

I looked at my hands. They were clean, but they had undone me. And I knew what would happen to the organization the minute I wasn't there, or became involved in this kind of trouble.

"Yes," I said. "I know. But what can I do?"

"Do you want to fight, or do you want to quit? You aren't the first guy in the world that ever got into a jam. What are you going to do about it? Are you going to put up a battle, or are you going to fold up?"

"If there's any chance at all, I'll take it."

"I wouldn't even know you, if I thought you'd do anything else."

"And of course, it's not only the organization, big as that is. There's my own neck, besides. Naturally, I'd like to save it."

Steve was matter of fact. "Of course. Now, what happened?"

"I can't describe it. I hardly know."

"Try."

"That bitch. Oh, God, Pauline."

"Yes?"

"She said that I, she actually accused both of us, but it's utterly fantastic. I had a few drinks and she must have had several. She said something about us. Can you take it?"

Steve was unmoved. "I know what she said. She would. And then?"

"That's all. I hit her over the head with something. A decanter. Maybe two or three times, maybe ten times. Yes, a decanter. I wiped my fingerprints off of it. She must have been insane, don't you think? To say a thing like that? She's a part-time Liz, Steve, did I ever tell you that?"

"You didn't have to."

"So I killed her. Before I even thought about it. God, I didn't intend anything like it, thirty seconds before. I don't understand it. And the organization is in trouble, real trouble. Did I tell you that?"

"You told me."

"I don't mean about this. I mean Carr and Wayne and—"

"You told me."

"Well, at dinner tonight I was sure of it. And now this. Oh, God."

"If you want to save the whole works you'll have to keep your head. And your nerve. Especially your nerve."

All at once, and for the first time in fifty years, my eyes were filled with tears. It was disgraceful. I could hardly see him. I said: "Don't worry about my nerve."

"That's talking," Steve said, evenly. "And now I want to hear the details. Who saw you go into this place, Pauline's apartment? Where was the doorman, the switchboard man? Who brought you there? Who took you away? I want to know every goddamn thing that happened, what she said to you and what you said to her. What she did and what you did. Where you were this evening, before you went to Pauline's. In the meantime, I'm going to lay out some clean clothes. You have bloodstains on your shirt and your trousers. I'll get rid of them. Meanwhile, go ahead."

"All right," I said, "I was having dinner at the Waynes'.

And they couldn't seem to talk about anything else except what a hell of a mess Janoth Enterprises was getting into. God, how they loved my difficulties. They couldn't think or talk about anything else."

"Skip that," said Steve. "Come to the point."

I told him about leaving the Waynes', how Bill had driven me to Pauline's.

"We don't have to worry about Bill," said Steve.

"God," I interrupted. "Do you really think I can get away with this?"

"You told me you wiped your fingerprints off the decanter, didn't you? What else were you thinking of when you did it?"

"That was automatic."

Steve waved the argument away.

"Talk."

I told him the rest of it. How I saw this stranger, leaving Pauline, and how we got into a quarrel in her apartment, and what she had said to me, and what I had said to her, and then what happened, as well as I remembered it.

Finally, Steve said to me: "Well, it looks all right except for one thing."

"What?"

"The fellow who saw you go into the building with Pauline. Nobody else saw you go in. But he did. Who was he?"

"I tell you, I don't know."

"Did he recognize you?"

"I don't know."

"The one guy in the world who saw you go into Pauline's apartment, and you don't know who he was? You don't know whether he knew you, or recognized you?"

"No, no, no. Why, is that important?"

Steve gave me a fathomless glance. He slowly found a cigarette, slowly reached for a match, lit the cigarette. When he blew out the second drag of smoke, still slowly, and thoughtfully blew out the match, and then put the burned match away and exhaled his third lungful, deliberately, he turned and said: "You're damned right it is. I want to hear everything there is to know about that guy." He flicked some ashes into a tray. "Everything. You may not know it, but he's the key to our whole set-up. In fact, Earl, he spells the difference. Just about the whole difference."

STEVE HAGEN

WE WENT over that evening forward and backward. We put every second of it under a high-powered microscope. Before we finished I knew as much about what happened as though I had been there myself, and that was a lot more than Earl did. This jam was so typical of him that, after the first blow, nothing about it really surprised me.

It was also typical that his simple mind could not wholly grasp how much was at stake and how much he had jeopardized it. Typical, too, that he had no idea how to control the situation. Nor how fast we had to work. Nor how.

Pauline's maid would not return to the apartment until tomorrow evening. There was a good chance the body would not be discovered until then. Then, Earl would be the first person seriously investigated by the police, since his connection with her was common knowledge.

I would have to claim he was with me throughout the dangerous period, and it would have to stick. But Billy would back that.

After leaving the Waynes', Earl had come straight here. Driven by Billy. Then Billy was given the rest of the night off. That was all right, quite safe.

There would be every evidence of Earl's frequent, former visits to Pauline's apartment, but nothing to prove the last one. Even I had gone there once or twice. She had lots of visitors running in and out, both men and women. But

I knew, from Earl's squeamish description, the injuries would rule out a woman.

The cover I had to provide for Earl would be given one hell of a going over. So would I. That couldn't be helped. It was my business, not only Earl's, and since he couldn't be trusted to protect our interests, I would have to do it myself.

Apparently it meant nothing to him, the prospect of going back to a string of garbage-can magazines edited from a due-bill office and paid for with promises, threats, rubber checks, or luck. He didn't even think about it. But I did. Earl's flair for capturing the mind of the reading public was far more valuable than the stuff they cram into banks. Along with this vision, though, he had a lot of whims, scruples, philosophical foibles, a sense of humor that he sometimes used even with me. These served some purpose at business conferences or social gatherings, but not now.

If necessary, if the situation got too hot, if Earl just couldn't take it, I might draw some of the fire myself. I could afford to. One of our men, Emory Mafferson, had phoned me here about the same time Earl was having his damned expensive tantrum. And that alibi was real.

The immediate problem, no matter how I turned it over, always came down to the big question mark of the stranger. No other living person had seen Earl, knowing him to be Earl, after he left that dinner party. For the tenth time, I asked: "There was nothing at all familiar about that person you saw?"

"Nothing. He was in a shadowy part of the street. With the light behind him."

"And you have no idea whether he recognized you?"

"No. But I was standing in the light of the entranceway. If he knew me, he recognized me."

Again I thought this over from every angle. "Or he may sometime recognize you," I concluded. "When he sees your face in the papers, as one of those being questioned. Maybe. And maybe we can take care they aren't good pictures. But I wish I had a line on that headache right now. Something to go on when the story breaks. So that we can always be a jump ahead of everyone, including the cops."

All I knew was that Pauline said the man's name was George Chester. This might even be his true name, though knowing Pauline, that seemed improbable, and the name was not listed in any of the phone books of the five boroughs, nor in any of the books of nearby suburbs. She said he was in advertising. That could mean anything. Nearly everyone was.

They had gone to a place on Third Avenue called Gil's, and for some reason it had seemed like an archeological foundation. This sounded authentic. The place could be located with no difficulty.

They had stopped in at a Third Avenue antique shop, and there the man had bought a picture, bidding for it against some woman who apparently just walked in from the street, as they did. It would not be hard to locate the shop and get more out of the proprietor. The picture was of a couple of hands. Its title, or subject matter, was something about Judas. The artist's name was Patterson. The canvas looked as though it came out of a dustbin. Then they had gone to the cocktail lounge of the Van Barth. It should not be hard to get another line on our character there. He certainly had the picture with him. He may even have checked it.

But the antique shop seemed a surefire bet. There would have been the usual long pointless talk about the picture. Even if the proprietor did not know either the man or the woman customer, he must have heard enough to offer new leads regarding the clown we wanted. The very fact he had gone into the place, then bought nothing except this thing, something that looked like it belonged in an incinerator, this already gave our bystander an individual profile. I said: "What kind of a person would do that, buy a mess like that in some hole-in-the-wall?"

"I don't know. Hell, I'd do it myself, if I felt like it."

"Well, I wouldn't feel like it. But there's another line. We can surely get a lead on the artist. We'll probably find a few clips in our own morgue. It's possible the man we are looking for is a great admirer of this artist, whoever he is. We can locate Patterson and get the history of this particular picture. Two hands. A cinch. There may be thousands, millions of these canvases around the city, but when you come right down to it, each of them has been seen by somebody besides the genius who painted it, and somebody would be certain to recognize it from a good description. After that, we can trace it along to the present owner."

Earl had by now come out of his first shock. He looked, acted, sounded, and thought more like his natural self. "How are we going to find this man, ahead of the police?" he asked.

"What have we got two thousand people for?"

"Yes, of course. But doesn't that mean—after all—isn't that spreading suspicion just that much farther?"

I had already thought of a way to put the organization in motion without connecting it at all with the death of Pauline.

"No. I know how to avoid that."

He thought that over for a while. Then he said: "Why

should you do this? Why do you stick your neck out? This is serious."

I knew him so well I had known, almost to the word, he would say that.

"I've done it before, haven't I? And more."

"Yes. I know. But I have a hell of a way of rewarding friendship like that. I merely seem to exact more of it. More risks. More sacrifices."

"Don't worry about me. You're the one who's in danger."

"I hope you're not. But I think you will be, giving me an alibi, and leading the search for this unknown party."

"I won't be leading the search. We want somebody else to do that. I stay in the background." I knew that Earl himself would go right on being our biggest headache. I thought it would be better to take the first hurdle now. "In the first place, I want to disassociate you from this business as far as possible. Don't you agree that's wise?" He nodded, and I slowly added, as an afterthought, "Then, when our comedian is located, we want an entirely different set of people to deal with him."

Earl looked up from the thick, hairy knuckles of the fingers he seemed to be studying. His face had never, even when he was most shaken, lost its jovial appearance. I wondered whether he had seemed to be smiling when he killed the woman, but of course he had been.

The question forming in that slow, unearthly mind of his at last boiled up. "By the way. What happens when we do locate this person?"

"That all depends. When the story breaks, he may go straight to the police. In that case our alibi stands, and our line is this: He says he saw you on the scene. What was he doing there, himself? That makes him as hot as you are.

We'll make him even warmer. We already know, for instance, that he spent a large part of the evening with Pauline."

Earl's round, large, staring eyes showed no understanding for a moment, then they came to life. "By God, Steve. I wonder—no. Of course you mean that only to threaten him off."

I said: "Put it this way. If the case goes to trial, and he persists in being a witness, that's the line we'll raise. Your own movements are accounted for, you were with me. But what was he doing there? What about this and that?—all the things we are going to find out about him long in advance. The case against you won't stand up."

Earl knew I had omitted something big, and in his mind he laboriously set out to find what it was. I waited while he thought it over, knowing he couldn't miss. Presently, he said: "All right. But if he doesn't go to the police the minute this breaks? Then what?"

I didn't want him to become even more hysterical, and if that were possible, I didn't want him to be even upset. I said, dispassionately: "If we find him first, we must play it safe."

"Well. What does that mean?"

Elaborately, I explained: "We could have him watched, of course. But we'd never know how much he actually did or did not realize, would we? And we certainly wouldn't know what he'd do next."

"Well? I can see that."

"Well. What is there to do with a man like that? He's a constant threat to your safety, your position in life, your place in the world. He's a ceaseless menace to your very life. Can you put up with an intolerable situation like that?"

Earl gave me a long, wondering, sick, almost frightened regard.

"I don't like that," he said, harshly. "There has already been one accident. I don't want another one. No. Not if I know what you mean."

"You know what I mean."

"No. I'm still a man."

"Are you? There are millions of dollars involved, all because of your uncontrollable temper and your God-forsaken stupidity. Yours, yours, not mine. Besides being an idiot, are you a coward, too?"

He floundered around for a cigar, got one, and with my help, finally got it going. Then, finally, he sounded a raw croak: "I won't see a man killed in cold blood." And as though he'd read my thoughts he added, "Nor take any part in it, either."

I said, reasonably: "I don't understand you. You know what kind of a world this is. You have always been a solid part of it. You know what anyone in Devers & Blair, Jennett-Donohue, Beacon, anyone above an M.E. in any of those houses would certainly do to you if he could reach out at night and safely push a button—"

"No. I wouldn't, myself. And I don't think they would, either."

He was wrong, of course, but there was no use arguing with a middle-aged child prodigy. I knew that by tomorrow he would see this thing in its true light.

"Well, it needn't come to that. That was just a suggestion. But why are you so worried? You and I have already seen these things happen, and we have helped to commit just about everything else for a lot less money. Why are you so sensitive now?"

He seemed to gag.

"Did we ever before go as far as this?"

"You were never in this spot before. Were you?" Now he looked really ghastly. He couldn't even speak. By God, he would have to be watched like a hawk and nursed every minute. "Let me ask you, Earl, are you ready to retire to a penitentiary and write your memoirs, for the sake of your morals? Or are you ready to grow up and be a man in a man's world, take your full responsibilities along with the rewards?" I liked Earl more than I had ever liked any person on earth except my mother, I really liked him, and I had to get both of us out of this at any cost. "No, we never went this far before. And we will never, if we use our heads, ever have to go this far again."

Earl absently drew at his cigar. "Death by poverty, famine, plague, war, I suppose that is on such a big scale the responsibility rests nowhere, although I personally have always fought against all of these things, in a number of magazines dedicated to wiping out each one of them, separately, and in some cases, in vehicles combating all of them together. But a personal death, the death of a definite individual. That is quite different."

He had reduced himself to the intellectual status of our own writers, a curious thing I had seen happen before. I risked it, and said: "We could take a chance on some simpler way, maybe. But there is more at stake than your private morals, personal philosophy, or individual life. The whole damned organization is at stake. If you're wiped out, so is that. When you go, the entire outfit goes. A flood of factory-manufactured nonsense swamps the market."

Earl stood up and paced slowly across the room. It was a long time before he answered me.

"I can be replaced, Steve. I'm just a cog. A good one, I know, but still only a cog."

This was better. This was more like it. I said, knowing him: "Yes, but when you break, a lot of others break, too. Whenever a big thing like this goes to pieces—and that is what could happen—a hell of a lot of innocent people, their plans, their homes, their dreams and aspirations, the future of their children, all of that can go to pieces with it. Myself, for instance."

He gave me one quick glance. But I had gambled that he was a sucker for the greatest good to the most people. And after a long, long while he spoke, and I knew that at heart he was really sound.

"Well, all right," he said. "I understand, Steve. I guess what has to be, has to be."

GEORGE STROUD VI

THE AWFULNESS of Monday morning is the world's great common denominator. To the millionaire and the coolie it is the same, because there can be nothing worse.

But I was only fifteen minutes behind the big clock when I sat down to breakfast, commenting that this morning's prunes had grown up very fast from the baby raisins in last night's cake. The table rhythmically shook and vibrated under Georgia's steadily drumming feet. It came to me again that a child drinking milk has the same vacant, contented expression of the well-fed cow who originally gave it. There is a real spiritual kinship there.

It was a fine sunny morning, like real spring, spring for keeps. I was beginning my second cup of coffee, and planning this year's gardening, when Georgette said: "George, have you looked at the paper? There's a dreadful story about a woman we met, I think. At Janoth's."

She waited while I picked up the paper. I didn't have to search. Pauline Delos had been found murdered. It was the leading story on page one.

Not understanding it, and not believing it, I read the headlines twice. But the picture was of Pauline.

The story said her body had been discovered at about noon on Sunday, and her death had been fixed at around ten o'clock on the night before. Saturday. I had left her at about that hour.

"Isn't that the same one?" Georgette asked.

"Yes," I said. "Yes."

She had been beaten to death with a heavy glass decanter. No arrest had been made. Her immediate friends were being questioned; Earl Janoth was one of them, the story went, but the publisher had not seen her for a number of days. He himself had spent the evening dining with acquaintances, and after dinner had spent several hours discussing business matters with an associate.

"A horrible story, isn't it?" said Georgette.

"Yes."

"Aren't you going to finish your coffee? George?"

"Yes?"

"You'd better finish your coffee, and then I'll drive you to the station."

"Yes. All right."

"Is something the matter?"

"No, of course not."

"Well, heavens. Don't look so grim."

I smiled.

"By the way," she went on. "I didn't tell you I liked that new picture you brought home. The one of the two hands. But it's in terrible condition, isn't it?"

"Yes, it is."

"It's another Patterson, isn't it?"

A hundred alarm bells were steadily ringing inside of me.

"Well, perhaps."

"Pity's sake, George, you don't have to be so monosyllabic, do you? Can't you say anything but 'yes,' 'no,' 'perhaps'? Is something the matter?"

"No. Nothing's the matter."

"Where did you get this new canvas?"

"Why, I just picked it up."

I knew quite well I had seen Earl entering that building

at ten o'clock on Saturday evening. She was alive when they passed into it. He now claimed he had not seen her for several days. Why? There could be only one answer.

But had he recognized me?

Whether he had or not, where did I stand? To become involved would bring me at once into the fullest and fiercest kind of spotlight. And that meant, to begin with, wrecking Georgette, Georgia, my home, my life.

It would also place me on the scene of the murder. That I did not like at all. Nothing would cover Janoth better.

Yet he almost surely knew someone had at least seen him there. Or did he imagine no one had?

"George?"

"Yes?"

"I asked you if you knew much about this Pauline Delos?"

"Very little."

"Goodness. You certainly aren't very talkative this morning."

I smiled again, swallowed the rest of my coffee, and said: "It is a ghastly business, isn't it?"

Somehow Georgia got packed off to school, and somehow I got down to the station. On the train going into town I read every newspaper, virtually memorizing what was known of the death, but gathering no real additional information.

At the office I went straight to my own room, and the moment I got there my secretary told me Steve Hagen had called and asked that I see him as soon as I got in.

I went at once to the thirty-second floor.

Hagen was a hard, dark little man whose soul had been hit by lightning, which he'd liked. His mother was a bank vault, and his father an International Business Machine. I knew he was almost as loyal to Janoth as to himself.

After we said hello and made about one casual remark, he said he would like me to undertake a special assignment.

"Anything you have on the fire downstairs at the moment," he said, "let it go. This is more important. Have you anything special, at this moment?"

"Nothing." Then because it could not be avoided, plausibly, I said: "By the way, I've just read about the Pauline Delos business. It's pretty damn awful. Have you any idea—?"

Steve's confirmation was short and cold. "Yes, it's bad. I have no idea about it."

"I suppose Earl is, well—"

"He is. But I don't really know any more about it than you do."

He looked around the top of his desk and located some notes. He raked them together, looked them over, and then turned again to me. He paused, in a way that indicated we were now about to go to work.

"We have a job on our hands, not hard but delicate, and it seems you are about the very best man on the staff to direct it." I looked at him, waiting, and he went on. "In essence, the job is this: We want to locate somebody unknown to us. Really, it's a missing person job." He waited again, and when I said nothing, he asked: "Would that be all right with you?"

"Of course. Who is it?"

"We don't know."

"Well?"

He ruffled his notes.

"The person we want went into some Third Avenue bar and grill by the name of Gil's last Saturday afternoon. He was accompanied by a rather striking blonde, also unidentified. They later went to a Third Avenue antique shop. In fact, several of them. But in one of them he bought a picture called *Judas*, or something to that effect. He bought the picture from the dealer, overbidding another customer, a woman who also wanted to buy it. The picture was by an artist named Patterson. According to the morgue," Steve Hagen pushed across a thin heavy-paper envelope from our own files, "this Louise Patterson was fairly well known ten or twelve years ago. You can read up on all that for yourself. But the picture bought by the man we want depicted two hands, I believe, and was in rather bad condition. I don't know what he paid for it. Later, he and the woman with him went to the cocktail lounge of the Van Barth for a few drinks. It is possible he checked the picture there, or he may have had it right with him."

No, I hadn't. I'd left it in the car. Steve stopped, and looked at me. My tongue felt like sandpaper. I asked: "Why do you want this man?"

Steve clasped his hands in back of his neck and gazed off into space, through the wide blank windows of the thirty-second floor. From where we sat, we could see about a hundred miles of New York and New Jersey countryside.

When he again turned to me he was a good self-portrait of candor. Even his voice was a good phonographic reproduction of the slightly confidential friend.

"Frankly, we don't know ourselves."

This went over me like a cold wind.

"You must have some idea. Otherwise, why bother?"

"Yes, we have an idea. But it's nothing definite. We think our party is an important figure, in fact a vital one, in a business and political conspiracy that has reached simply colossal proportions. Our subject is not necessarily a big fellow in his own right, but we have reason to believe he's the payoff man between an industrial syndicate and a political machine, the one man who really knows the entire set-up. We believe we can crack the whole situation, when we find him."

So Earl had gone straight to Hagen. Hagen would then be the business associate who provided the alibi. But what did they want with George Stroud?

It was plain Earl knew he had been seen, and afraid he had been recognized. I could imagine how he would feel.

"Pretty vague, Steve," I said. "Can't you give me more?"

"No. You're right, it is vague. Our information is based entirely on rumors and tips and certain, well, striking coincidences. When we locate our man, then we'll have something definite for the first time."

"What's in it? A story for *Crimeways?*"

Hagen appeared to give that question a good deal of thought. He said, finally, and with apparent reluctance: "I don't think so. I don't know right now what our angle will be when we have it. We might want to give it a big play in one of our books, eventually. Or we might decide to use it in some entirely different way. That's up in the air."

I began to have the shadowy outline of a theory. I tested it.

"Who else is in on this? Should we co-operate with anyone? The cops, for instance?"

Cautiously, and with regret, Steve told me: "Absolutely not. This is our story, exclusively. It must stay that way. You will have to go to other agencies for information, naturally. But you get it only, you don't give it. Is that perfectly clear?"

It was beginning to be. "Quite clear."

"Now, do you think you can knock together a staff, just as large as you want, and locate this person? The only additional information I have is that his name may be George Chester, and he's of average build and height, weight one-forty to one-eighty. It's possible he's in advertising. But your best lead is this place called Gil's, the shop where he bought the picture, and the bar of the Van Barth. And that picture, perhaps the artist. I have a feeling the picture alone might give us the break."

"It shouldn't be impossible," I said.

"We want this guy in a hurry. Can you do it?"

If I didn't, someone else would. It would have to be me.

"I've done it before."

"Yes. That's why you're elected."

"What do I do when I find this person?"

"Nothing." Steve's voice was pleasant, but emphatic. "Just let me know his name, and where he can be found. That's all."

It was like leaning over the ledge of one of these thirty-second floor windows and looking down into the street below. I always had to take just one more look.

"What happens when we locate him? What's the next step?"

"Just leave that to me." Hagen stared at me, coldly and levelly, and I stared back. I saw, in those eyes, there was no room for doubt at all. Janoth knew the danger he was in, Hagen knew it, and for Hagen there was literally no limit. None. Furthermore, this little stick of dynamite was intelligent, and he had his own ways, his private means.

"Now, this assignment has the right-of-way over everything, George. You can raid any magazine, use any bureau, any editor or correspondent, all the resources we have. And you're in charge."

I stood up and scooped together the notes I had taken. The squeeze felt tangible as a vise. My personal life would be destroyed if I ran to the cops. Death if Hagen and his special friends caught up with me.

"All right, Steve," I said. "I take it I have absolute carte blanche."

"You have. Expense, personnel, everything." He waved toward the windows overlooking about ten million people. "Our man is somewhere out there. It's a simple job. Get him."

I looked out of the windows myself. There was a lot of territory out there. A nation within a nation. If I picked the right kind of a staff, twisted the investigation where I could, jammed it where I had to, pushed it hard where it was safe, it might be a very, very, very long time before they found George Stroud.

GEORGE STROUD VII

I HATED to interrupt work on the coming issues of our own book, and so I decided to draw upon all the others, when needed, as evenly as possible.

But I determined to work Roy into it. Bert Finch, Tony, Nat, Sydney, and the rest of them would never miss either of us. And although I liked Roy personally, I could also count upon him to throw a most complicated monkey-wrench into the simplest mechanism. Leon Temple, too, seemed safe enough. And Edward Orlin of *Futureways*, a plodding, rather wooden esthete, precisely unfitted for the present job. He would be working for George Stroud, in the finest sense.

I told Roy about the new assignment, explained its urgency, and then I put it up to him. I simply had to have someone in charge at the office, constantly. This might be, very likely would be, a round-the-clock job. That meant there would have to be another man to share the responsibility.

Roy was distantly interested, and even impressed. "This takes precedence over everything?"

I nodded.

"All right. I'm in. Where do we start?"

"Let me line up the legmen first. Then we'll see."

Fifteen minutes later I had the nucleus of the staff gathered in my office. In addition to Roy and Leon, there were seven men and two women drawn from other magazines and departments. Edward Orlin, rather huge and dark and fat; Phillip Best of *Newsways,* a small, acrid, wire-haired encyclopedia. The two women, Louella Metcalf and Janet Clark, were included if we needed feminine reserves. Louella, drawn from *The Sexes,* was a tiny, earnest, appealing creature, the most persistent and transparent liar I have ever known. Janet was a very simple, eager, large-boned brunette whose last assignment had been with *Homeways;* she did every job about four times over, eventually doing it very well. Don Klausmeyer of *Personalities* and Mike Felch of *Fashions* had also been conscripted, and one man each from *Commerce, Sportland,* and the auditing department. They would do for a convincing start.

From now on, everything would have to look good. Better than good. Perfect. I gave them a crisp, businesslike explanation.

"You are being asked to take on a unique and rather strange job," I said. "It has to be done quickly, and as quietly as possible. I know you can do it.

"We have been given a blank check as far as the resources of the organization are concerned. If you need help on your particular assignment, help of any sort, you can have it. If it's a routine matter, simply go to the department that can give it. If it's something special, come either to me, or to Roy, here, who will be in charge of the work whenever for some reason I have to be elsewhere myself.

"We are looking for somebody. We don't know much about this person, who he is, where he lives. We don't even know his name. His name may be George Chester, but that is doubtful. It is possible he is in the advertising business, and that will be your job, Harry." I said this to Harry Slater, the fellow from *Commerce.* "You will comb the advertising agencies, clubs, if necessary the advertising

[92]

departments of first the metropolitan newspapers and magazines, then those farther out. If you have to go that far, you will need a dozen or so more men to help you. You are in complete charge of that line of investigation." Harry's inquiries were safe, and they could also be impressive. I added: "Take as many people as you need. Cross-check with us regularly, for the additional information about our man that will be steadily coming in from all the other avenues we will be exploring at the same time. And that applies to all of you.

"We not only don't know this man's right name or where he lives—and that will be your job, Alvin." This was Alvin Dealey, from the auditing department. "Check all real estate registers in this area, all tax records, public utilities, and all phone books of cities within, say, three or four hundred miles, for George Chester, and any other names we give you. Take as many researchers as you need.

"Now, as I said, we not only don't know this man's name or whereabouts, but we haven't even got any kind of a physical description of him. Just that he is of average height, say five nine to eleven, and average build. Probably between one-forty and one-eighty.

"But there are a few facts we have to go upon. He is an habitue of a place on Third Avenue called Gil's. Here is a description of the place." I gave it, but stayed strictly within the memo as given by Steve Hagen. "This man was in that place, wherever it is, last Saturday afternoon. At that time he was there with a woman we know to be a good-looking blonde. Probably he goes there regularly. That will be your job, Ed. You will find this restaurant, night club, saloon, or whatever it is, and when you do you will stay there until our man comes into it." Ed Orlin's swarthy and rather flabby face betrayed, just for an instant, amazement and incipient distaste.

"On the same evening our subject went into an antique shop, also on Third Avenue. He went into several, but there is one in particular we want, which shouldn't be hard to find. You will find it, Phil. Because the fellow we are looking for bought a picture, unframed, while he was in the place, and he bought it after outbidding another customer, a woman." I did not elaborate by a hairsbreadth beyond Steve's written memo. "The canvas was by an artist named Louise Patterson, it depicted two hands, was in bad condition, and the name of it, or the subject matter, had something to do with Judas. The dealer is certain to remember the incident. You can get an accurate description of our man from him. Perhaps he knows him, and can give us his actual identity.

"Don, here is our file on this Louise Patterson. There is a possibility that this picture can be traced from the artist to the dealer and from him to our unknown. Look up Patterson, or if she's dead, look up her friends. Somebody will remember that canvas, what became of it, may even know who has it now. Find out." I had suddenly the sick and horrid realization I would have to destroy that picture. "Perhaps the man we are looking for is an art collector, even a Patterson enthusiast.

"Leon, I want you and Janet to go to the bar of the Van Barth, where this same blonde went with this same person, on the same evening. At that time he had the picture, and perhaps he checked it. Find out. Question the bartenders, the checkroom attendants for all they can give you regarding the man, and then I guess you'd better stay right there and wait for him to turn up, since he's probably a regular there, as well as Gil's. You may have to be around for several days and if so you will have to be relieved by Louella and Dick Englund."

Leon and Janet looked as though they might not care to be relieved, while Louella and Dick perceptibly brightened. It was almost a pleasure to dispense such largesse. I wished them many a pleasant hour while they awaited my arrival.

"That is about all I have to give you now," I concluded. "Do you all understand your immediate assignments?" Apparently, the lieutenants in charge of the hunt for George Stroud all did, for none of them said anything. "Well, are there any questions?"

Edward Orlin had one. "Why are we looking for this man?"

"All I know about that," I said, "is the fact that he is the intermediary figure in one of the biggest political-industrial steals in history. That is, he is the connecting link, and we need him to establish the fact of this conspiracy. Our man is the payoff man."

Ed Orlin took this information and seemed to retire behind a wall of thought to eat and digest it. Alvin Dealey earnestly asked: "How far can we go in drawing upon the police for information?"

"You can draw upon them, but you are not to tell them anything at all," I said, flatly. "This is our story, in the first place, and we intend to keep it ours. In the second place, I told you there is a political tie-up here. The police machinery we go to may be all right at one end, ours, but we don't know and we have no control over the other end of that machine. Is that clear?"

Alvin nodded. And then the shrewd, rather womanish voice of Phillip Best cut in. "All of these circumstances you have given us concern last Saturday," he said. "That was the night Pauline Delos was killed. Everyone knows what that means. Is there any connection?"

"Not as far as I know, Phil," I said. "This is purely a big-time business scandal that Hagen himself and a few others have been digging into for some time past. Now, it's due to break." I paused for a moment, to let this very thin logic take what hold it could. "As far as I understand it, Earl intends to go through with this story, regardless of the ghastly business last Saturday night."

Phil's small gray eyes bored through his rimless glasses. "I just thought, it's quite a coincidence," he said. I let that pass without even looking at it, and he added: "Am I to make inquiries about the woman who was with the man?"

"You will all have to do that." I had no doubt of what they would discover. Yet even delay seemed in my favor, and I strongly reminded them, "But we are not looking for the woman, or any other outside person. It is the man we want, and only the man."

I let my eyes move slowly over them, estimating their reactions. As far as I could see, they accepted the story. More important, they seemed to give credit to my counterfeit assurance and determination.

"All right," I said. "If there are no more questions, suppose you intellectual tramps get the hell out of here and go to work." As they got up, reviewing the notes they had taken, and stuffed them into their pockets, I added, "And don't fail to report back, either in person or by phone. Soon, and often. Either to Roy or myself."

When they had all gone, except Roy, he got up from his chair beside me at the desk. He walked around in front of it, then crossed to the wall facing it, hands thrust into his pockets. He leaned against the wall, staring at the carpet. Presently, he said: "This is a crazy affair. I can't help feeling that Phil somehow hit the nail on the head. There is a curious connection there, I'm certain, the fact that all of this happened last Saturday."

I waited, with a face made perfectly blank.

"I don't mean it has any connection with that frightful business about Pauline Delos," he went on, thoughtfully. "Of course it hasn't. That would be a little too obvious. But I can't help thinking that something, I don't know what, something happened last week on Friday or Saturday, perhaps while Janoth was in Washington, or certainly a few days before, or even last night, Sunday, that would really explain why we are looking for this mysterious, art-collecting stranger at this moment, and in such a hurry. Don't you think so?"

"Sounds logical," I said.

"Damn right it's logical. It seems to me, we would do well to comb the outstanding news items of the last two weeks, particularly the last five or six days, and see what there is that might concern Janoth. This Jennett-Donohue proposition, for instance. Perhaps they are actually planning to add those new books in our field. That would seriously bother Earl, don't you think?"

Roy was all right. He was doing his level best.

"You may be right. And again it may be something else, far deeper, not quite so apparent. Suppose you follow up that general line? But at the same time, I can't do anything except work from the facts supplied to me."

Actually, I was at work upon a hazy plan that seemed a second line of defense, should it come to that. It amounted to a counterattack. The problem, if the situation got really bad, was this: How to place Janoth at the scene of the killing, through some third, independent witness, or through evidence not related to myself. Somewhere in that fatal detour his car had been noted, he himself had been seen and marked. If I had to fight fire with fire, somehow, surely he could be connected.

But it would never come to that. The gears being shifted, the wheels beginning to move in this hunt for me were big and smooth and infinitely powered, but they were also blind. Blind, clumsy, and unreasoning. "No, you have to work with the data you've been given," Roy admitted. "But I think it would be a good idea if I did follow up my hunch. I'll see if we haven't missed something in recent political developments."

At the same time that I gave him silent encouragement, I became aware of the picture above his head on the wall against which he leaned. It was as though it had suddenly screamed.

Of course. I had forgotten I had placed that Patterson there, two years ago. I had bought it at the Lewis Galleries, the profiles of two faces, showing only the brow, eyes, nose, lips, and chin of each. They confronted each other, distinctly Pattersonian. One of them showed an avaricious, the other a skeptical leer. I believe she had called it *Study in Fury*.

It was such a familiar landmark in my office that to take it away, now, would be fatal. But as I looked at it and then looked away I really began to understand the danger in which I stood. It would have to stay there, though at any moment someone might make a connection. And there must be none, none at all, however slight.

"Yes," I told Roy, automatically, feeling the after-shock in fine points of perspiration all over me. "Why not do that? We may have missed something significant in business changes, as well as politics."

"I think it might simplify matters," he said, and moved

away from the wall on which the picture hung. "Janoth was in Washington this week end, remember. Personally, I think there's a tie-up between that and this rush order we've been given."

Thoughtfully, Roy moved away from the wall, crossed the thickly carpeted floor, disappeared through the door leading to his own office.

When he had gone I sat for a long moment, staring at that thing on the wall. I had always liked it before.

But no. It had to stay there.

EDWARD ORLIN

G IL'S TAVERN looked like just a dive on the outside, and also on the inside. Too bad I couldn't have been assigned to the Van Barth. Well, it couldn't be helped.

It was in the phone book, and not far off, so that part of it was all right. I walked there in twenty minutes.

I took along a copy of *War and Peace*, which I was re-reading, and on the way I saw a new issue of *The Creative Quarterly*, which I bought.

It was a little after one o'clock when I got there, time for lunch, so I had it. The food was awful. But it would go on the expense account, and after I'd eaten I got out my notebook and put it down. Lunch, $1.50. Taxi, $1.00. I thought for a minute, wondering what Stroud would do if he ever came to a dive like this, then I added: Four high-balls, $2.00.

After I'd finished my coffee and a slab of pie at least three days old I looked around. It was something dug up by an archeological expedition, all right. There was saw-dust in the corners, and a big wreath on the wall in back of me, celebrating a recent banquet, I suppose: CON-GRATULATIONS TO OUR PAL.

Then I saw the bar at the end of the long room. It was incredible. It looked as though a whole junkyard had been scooped up and dumped there. I saw wheels, swords, shovels, tin cans, bits of paper, flags, pictures, literally hundreds upon hundreds of things, just things.

After I paid for the 85¢ lunch, a gyp, and already I had

[100]

indigestion, I picked up my Tolstoy and *The Creative Quarterly* and walked down to the bar.

The nearer I came to it the more things I saw, simply thousands of them. I sat down and noticed there was a big fellow about fifty years old, with staring, preoccupied eyes, in back of it. He came down the bar, and I saw that his eyes were looking at me but didn't quite focus. They were like dim electric lights in an empty room. His voice was a wordless grunt.

"A beer," I said. I noticed that he spilled some of it when he put the glass down in front of me. His face really seemed almost ferocious. It was very strange, but none of my business. I had work to do. "Say, what've you got in back of the bar there? Looks like an explosion in a five-and-ten-cent store."

He didn't say anything for a couple of seconds, just looked me over, and now he seemed really sore about something.

"My personal museum," he said, shortly.

So that was what the memo meant. I was in the right place, no doubt about it.

"Quite a collection," I said. "Buy you a drink?"

He had a bottle on the bar by the time I finished speaking. Scotch, and one of the best brands, too. Well, it was a necessary part of the assignment. Made no difference to me; it went on the expense account.

He dropped the first jigger he picked up, left it where it fell, and only finally managed to fill the second one. But he didn't seem drunk. Just nervous.

"Luck," he said. He lifted the glass and the whisky was all gone, in five seconds, less than five seconds, almost in a flash. When he put down the jigger and picked up the bill I laid on the bar he noisily smacked his lips. "First of the day," he said. "That's always the best. Except for the last."

I sipped my beer, and when he laid down the change, he was charging 75¢ for his own Scotch, I said: "So that's your personal museum. What's in it?"

He turned and looked at it and he sounded much better. "Everything. You name it and I've got it. What's more, it's an experience what happened to me or my family."

"Sort of a petrified autobiography, is that it?"

"No, just my personal museum. I been around the world six times, and my folks before me been all over it. Farther than that. Name me one thing I haven't got in that museum, and the drinks are on me."

It was fantastic. I didn't see how I'd ever get any information out of this fellow. He was an idiot.

"All right," I said, humoring him. "Show me a locomotive."

He muttered something that sounded like, "Locomotive? Now, where did that locomotive get to." Then he reached away over in back of a football helmet, a stuffed bird, a bowl heaped to the brim with foreign coins, and a lot of odds and ends I couldn't even see, and when he turned around he laid a toy railroad engine on the bar. "This here locomotive," he confided, slapping it affectionately and leaning toward me, "was the only toy of mine what got saved out of the famous Third Avenue fire next to the carbarns fifty years ago. Saved it myself. I was six years old. They had nine roasts."

I finished my beer and stared at him, not sure whether he was trying to kid me or whether he was not only half drunk but completely out of his mind besides. If it was supposed to be humor, it was certainly corny, the incredibly childish slapstick stuff that leaves me cold. Why couldn't I have gotten the Van Barth, where I could at least read in peace and comfort, without having to interview a schizophrenic, probably homicidal.

"That's fine," I said.

"Still runs, too," he assured me, and gave the key a twist, put the toy down on the bar, and let it run a few feet. It stopped when it bumped into *The Creative Review*. He actually sounded proud. "See? Still runs."

God, this was simply unbelievable. I might as well be back in the office.

The lunatic gravely put the toy back behind the bar, where I heard its spring motor expend itself, and when he turned around he wordlessly filled up our glasses again, mine with beer and his with Scotch. I was still more surprised when he tossed off his drink, then returned and absently paused in front of me, appearing to wait. For God's sake, did this fellow expect a free drink with every round? Not that it mattered. He had to be humored, I suppose. After I'd paid, and by now he seemed actually friendly, he asked: "Yes, sir. That's one of the best private museums in New York. Anything else you'd care to see?"

"You haven't got a crystal ball, have you?"

"Well, now, as it happens, I have." He brought out a big glass marble from a pile of rubbish surmounted by a crucifix and a shrunken head. "Funny how everybody wants to see that locomotive, or sometimes it's the airplane or the steamroller, and usually they ask to see the crystal ball. Now this here little globe I picked up in Calcutta. I went to a Hindu gypsy what told fortunes, and he seen in the glass that I was in danger of drowning. So I jumped the ship I was on and went on the beach awhile, and not two days passed before that boat went down with all hands. So I says to myself, Holy Smoke, how long's this been going on? I never put much stock in that stuff before, see? So I went back to this fellow, and I says, I'd like to have that there gadget. And he says, in his own language of course, this been in his family for generations after generations and he can't part with it."

This juvenile nonsense went on and on. My God, I thought it would never stop. And I had to look as though I were interested. Finally it got so boring I couldn't stand any more of it. I said: "Well, I wish you'd look into that globe and see if you can locate a friend of mine for me."

"That's a funny thing. When I finally paid the two thousand rupees he wanted, and I took it back to my hotel, I couldn't make the damn thing work. And never could since."

"Never mind," I said. "Have another drink." He put the marble away and drew another beer and poured himself another Scotch. I couldn't see how a fellow like this stayed in business for more than a week.

Before he could put his drink away I went on: "A friend of mine I haven't seen for years comes in here sometimes, and I wonder if you know him. I'd like to see him again. Maybe you know what would be a good time to find him here."

The man's eyes went absolutely blank.

"What's his name?"

"George Chester."

"George Chester." He stared at the far end of the room, apparently thinking, and a little of the mask fell away from him. "That name I don't know. Mostly, I don't know their names, anyway. What's he look like?"

"Oh, medium height and build," I said. "A mutual acquaintance told me he saw him in here late last Saturday afternoon. With a good-looking blonde."

He threw the shot of whisky into his mouth and I don't

believe the glass even touched his lips. Didn't this fellow ever take a chaser? He frowned and paused.

"I think I know who you mean. Clean-cut, brown-haired fellow?"

"I guess you could call him that."

"I remember that blonde. She was something for the books. She wanted to see the raven that fellow wrote about, nevermore quoth he. So I let her have a look at it. Yes, they were in here a couple of nights ago, but he don't come around here very often. Four or five years ago he was in here lots, almost every night. Smart, too. Many's the time I used to show him my museum, until me and some hacker had to pick him up and carry him out. One night he wouldn't go home at all, he wanted to sleep right inside the museum. 'Book me the royal suite on your ocean liner, Gil,' he kept saying. We got him home all right. But that was several years ago." He looked at me with sharp interest. "Friend of yours?"

I nodded. "We used to work for the same advertising agency."

He puzzled some more. "I don't think he did then," he decided. "He worked for some newspaper, and before that he and his wife used to run a joint upstate, the same as mine. No museum, of course. Seems to me his name might have been George Chester, at that. I had to garage his car once or twice when he had too much. But he gradually stopped coming in. I don't think he was here more than twice in the last three or four months. But he might come in any time, you never can tell. Very intelligent fellow. What they call eccentric."

"Maybe I could reach him through the blonde."

"Maybe."

"Who is she, do you know?"

This time his whole face went blank. "No idea, sir."

He moved up the bar to serve some customers who had just entered, and I opened *The Creative Review*. There was a promising revaluation of Henry James I would have to read, though I knew the inevitable shortcomings of the man who wrote it. A long article on Tibetan dance ritual that looked quite good.

I finished my beer and went to a phone booth. I called the office and asked for Stroud, but got Cordette instead.

"Where's Stroud?" I asked.

"Out. Who's this?"

"Ed Orlin. I'm at Gil's Tavern."

"Found it, did you? Get the right one?"

"It's the right one, no question. And what a dive."

"Pick up anything?"

"Our man was here last Saturday, all right, and with the blonde."

"Fine. Let's have it."

"There isn't much. The bartender isn't sure of his name, because the guy doesn't come in here any more." I let that sink in, for a moment. I certainly hoped to get called off this drab saloon and that boring imbecile behind the bar. "But he thinks his name may actually be George Chester. He has been described by the bartender, who is either a half-wit or an outright lunatic himself, as very intelligent and eccentric. Believe me, Chester is probably just the opposite."

"Why?"

"It's that kind of a place. Eccentric, yes, but only a moron would come into a dump like this and spend hours talking to the fellow that runs this menagerie."

"Go on."

"The physical description we have does not seem far

wrong, but there's nothing to add to it, except that he's brown-haired and clean-cut."

"All right. What else? Any line on the blonde?"

"Nothing."

"That certainly isn't much, is it?"

"Well, wait. Our man is unquestionably a dipsomaniac. Four or five years ago he was in here every night and had to be sent home in a taxi. At that time he was a newspaperman, the bartender believes, and he never heard of him as working for an advertising concern. And before he was a newspaperman he ran a tavern somewhere upstate, with his wife."

"A drunk. Formerly, with his wife, a tavern proprietor. Probably a newspaperman, eccentric, clean-cut in appearance. It isn't much, but it's something. Is that all?"

"That's all. And our baby hasn't been in here more than twice in the last eight or ten months. So what should I do? Come back to the office?"

There was a pause, and I had a moment of hope.

"I think not, Ed. He was in there two days ago, he might not wait so long before he returns. And you can work on the bartender some more. Psychoanalyze him for more details. Have a few drinks with him."

Oh, my God.

"Listen, this fellow is a human blotter."

"All right, get drunk with him, if you have to. But not too drunk. Try some of the other customers. Anyway, stick around until we call you back, or send a relief. What's the address and the phone number?"

I gave them to him.

"All right, Ed. And if you get anything more, call us at once. Remember, this is a hurry-up job."

I hoped so. I went back to the bar, already a little dizzy

on the beers. It would be impossible to concentrate on the magazine, which demanded an absolutely clear head. One of the customers was roaring at the bartender, "All right, admit you ain't got it. I ask you, show me a *mot de passe* out of that famous museum, so-called."

"No double-talk allowed. You want to see something, you got to ask for it in plain language."

"That is plain language. Plain, ordinary French. Admit it, and give us a beer. You just ain't got one."

"All right, all right, I'll give you a beer. But what is this here thing? How do you spell it? Only don't ask for nothing in French again. Not in here, see?"

Well, there was a newspaper at the end of the bar, thank God. This morning's, but it could kill a couple of hours.

GEORGE STROUD VIII

WHEN they all cleared out of my office on their various assignments, I called in Emory Mafferson. His plump face was in perpetual mourning, his brain was a seething chaos, his brown eyes seemed always trying to escape from behind those heavy glasses, and I don't believe he could see more than ten feet in front of him, but somewhere in Emory I felt there was a solid newspaperman and a lyric investigator.

"How are you coming along with Funded Individuals?" I asked him.

"All right. I've explained it all to Bert, and we're finishing the article together."

"Sure Bert understands it?"

Emory's face took a turn for the worse.

"As well as I do," he finally said. "Maybe better. You know, I can't help feeling there's something sound in back of that idea. It's a new, revolutionary vision in the field of social security."

"Well, what's troubling you?"

"How can you have a revolution without a revolution?"

"Just leave that to Bert Finch. He has your *Futureways* notes, and he can interpret the data as far as you've gone with it. Suppose you let Bert carry on alone from here?"

Emory sighed.

If I understood him, many an afternoon supposedly spent in scholarly research at the library or interviewing some insurance expert had found him instead at Belmont, the Yankee Stadium, possibly home in bed.

"All good things have to come to an end sometime, Emory."

"I suppose so."

I came abruptly to the point. "Right now I have got to work on a special, outside job. At the same time, one of the most sensational murders of the year has occurred, and beyond a doubt it will assume even greater proportions and sometime *Crimeways* will want a big story about it."

"Delos?"

I nodded.

"And I don't want *Crimeways* left at the post. You wanted to go on our regular staff. This can start you off. Suppose you go down to Center Street, Homicide Bureau, and pick up everything you can, as and when it happens. The minute you've got it, phone it to me. I'll be busy with this other assignment, but I want to be up-to-date on the Delos story, every phase of it."

Emory looked more stunned and haggard than ever. Those brown goldfish eyes swam three times around the bowl of his glasses.

"God, you don't expect me to break this thing alone, do you?"

"Of course not. If we wanted to break it, we'd give it a big play, thirty or forty legmen. I just want all the facts ready when the case is broken, by the cops. All you have to do is keep in close touch with developments. And report back to me, and only me, regularly. Got it?"

Emory looked relieved, and said he understood. He got up to go. My private detective force wasn't much bigger standing than sitting, and looked even less impressive.

"What have you got for me to go on?" he asked.

"Nothing. Just what you have, no more."

"Will this be all right with Bert?"

I said I'd arrange that, and sent him on his way. After he'd gone I sat and looked at that Patterson *Study in Fury* on the opposite wall, facing me, and did nothing but think.

The signature was quite visible, and even moving the canvas downward into the lower part of the frame would not obscure it. I did not believe it possible, but there might, also, be others in the Janoth organization who would recognize a Patterson simply from the style.

I could not remove that picture. Even if I changed it for another, the change would be noticed by someone. Maybe not by Roy, the writers, or the reporters, but by someone. Lucille or one of the other girls, somebody else's secretary, some research worker.

If only that picture weren't there. And above all, if only I had never brought home *The Temptation of St. Judas.*

Because Georgette had seen the new picture.

Hagen was certain whoever had bought it could be traced through it. If he thought it necessary, he would insist upon a far more intensive search for it than the one I had, as a safeguard, assigned Don Klausmeyer to undertake. I knew Don would never trace it clear through from the artist to the dealer, let alone to me. But Hagen might at any moment take independent steps; I could think of some, myself, that would be dangerous.

I had better destroy the *Temptation.*

If somebody did his job too well, if Hagen went to work on his own, if some real information got to him before I could short-circuit it, that thing would nail me cold. I must get rid of it.

I put on my hat and went into Roy's office, with two half-formed ideas, to destroy that picture now and to find a means of locating Earl Janoth at 58 East through other witnesses. I could trust no one but myself with either of these jobs.

"I'm going out on a lead, Roy," I told him. "Take over for a while. And by the way, I've assigned somebody to follow the Delos murder. We'll want to handle it in an early issue, don't you think?" He nodded thoughtfully. "I've assigned Mafferson."

He nodded again, dryly and remotely. "I believe Janoth will want it followed, at least," he said. "By the way, I'm having the usual missing-person index prepared."

This was a crisscross of the data that came in, as rapidly as it came, simplified for easy reference. I had myself, at one time or another, helped to simplify it.

Over my shoulder I said, briskly: "That's the stuff."

I went out to the elevators, rode down and crossed the street to the garage. I decided to get the car, drive out to Marble Road and burn up that business right now.

In the garage, I met Earl Janoth's chauffeur, Billy, coming out of it. He had just brought in Janoth's car. I had ridden in it perhaps a dozen times, and now he nodded, impassively pleasant.

"Hello, Mr. Stroud."

"Hello, Billy."

We passed each other, and I felt suddenly cold and aware. There were two people Janoth trusted without limit, Steve Hagen and Billy, his physical shadow. When and if the missing unknown was located, Billy would be the errand boy sent to execute the final decision. He would be the man. He didn't know it, but I knew it.

Inside the garage an attendant was polishing Janoth's already shining Cadillac. I walked up to him, memorizing the car's license. Somebody else, somewhere, had seen it that night, and Earl, I hoped, and seen them where they were not supposed to be.

"Want your car, Mr. Stroud?"

I said hello and told him I did. I had often stopped for a minute or two with this particular attendant, talking about baseball, horses, whisky, or women.

"Got a little errand to do this afternoon," I said, and then gave him a narrow smile. "I'll bet this bus is giving you plenty of trouble."

I got a knowing grin in return.

"Not exactly trouble," he confided. "But the cops have been giving it a going over. Us too. Was it cleaned since Saturday night? How long was it out Saturday night? Did I notice the gas, the mileage, anything peculiar? Hell, we guys never pay any attention to things like that. Except, of course, we know it wasn't washed, and it wasn't even gassed."

He called to another attendant to bring down my car, and while I waited for it, I asked: "I suppose the cops third degree'd the chauffeur?"

"Sure. A couple of them tackled him again a few minutes ago. But the driver's got nothing to worry about. Neither has Mr. Janoth. They drove to a dinner somewhere and then they drove straight to some other place. Your friend Mr. Hagen's. It checks okay with us. They never garage this car here nights or week ends, so what would we know about it? But I don't mind cops. Only, I don't like that driver. Nothing I could say, exactly. Just, well."

He looked at me and I gave him an invisible signal in return and then my car was brought down.

I got into it and drove off, toward Marble Road. But

I hadn't gone more than three blocks before I began to think it all over again, and this time in a different mood.

Why should I destroy that picture? I liked it. It was mine.

Who was the better man, Janoth or myself? I voted for myself. Why should I sacrifice my own property just because of him? Who was he? Only another medium-sized wheel in the big clock.

The big clock didn't like pictures, much. I did. This particular picture it had tossed into the dustbin. I had saved it from oblivion, myself. Why should I throw it back?

There were lots of good pictures that were prevented from being painted at all. If they couldn't be aborted, or lost, then somebody like me was despatched to destroy them.

Just as Billy would be sent to destroy me. And why should I play ball in a deadly set-up like that?

What would it get me to conform?

Newsways, Commerce, Crimeways, Personalities, The Sexes, Fashions, Futureways, the whole organization was full and overrunning with frustrated ex-artists, scientists, farmers, writers, explorers, poets, lawyers, doctors, musicians, all of whom spent their lives conforming, instead. And conforming to what? To a sort of overgrown, aimless, haphazard stenciling apparatus that kept them running to psychoanalysts, sent them to insane asylums, gave them high blood pressure, stomach ulcers, killed them off with cerebral hemorrhages and heart failure, sometimes suicide. Why should I pay still more tribute to this fatal machine? It would be easier and simpler to get squashed stripping its gears than to be crushed helping it along.

To hell with the big gadget. I was a dilettante by profession. A pretty good one, I had always thought. I decided to stay in that business.

I turned down a side street and drove toward 58 East. I could make a compromise. That picture could be put out of circulation, for the present. But it would really be a waste of time to destroy it. That would mean only a brief reprieve, at best. Its destruction was simply not worth the effort.

And I could beat the machine. The super-clock would go on forever, it was too massive to be stopped. But it had no brains, and I did. I could escape from it. Let Janoth, Hagen, and Billy perish in its wheels. They loved it. They liked to suffer. I didn't.

I drove past 58 East, and began to follow the course the other car must have taken going away. Either Janoth had dismissed Billy when he arrived, and returned by taxi, or he had ordered Billy to come back later. In any case, Janoth had dined at the Waynes', according to all accounts, and then, as I knew, he had come to 58 East, and then of course he must have gone directly to Hagen's.

I followed the logical route to Hagen's. I saw two nearby cabstands. Janoth must have used one of them if he had returned by taxi, unless he had found a cruising cab somewhere between the two. He certainly would not have been so stupid as to pick one up near 58 East.

The farthest cabstand was the likeliest. I could begin there, with a photograph of Janoth, then try the nearer, and if necessary I could even check the bigger operators for cruisers picking up fares in the neighborhood on that evening. But that was a tall order for one man to cover.

From Hagen's, timing the drive, I went to the Waynes', then turned around and drove slowly back to 58 East. The route Earl must have followed took about thirty minutes.

Allowing another thirty minutes for the fight to develop, that meant Earl was covering up about one hour. This checked with the facts known to me.

Perhaps he had stopped somewhere along the way, but if so, no likely place presented itself.

That gave me only two possible leads, a cab by which Earl may have made his getaway, or possibly some attendant at Pauline's or Hagen's.

It was pretty slim. But something.

I drove back to the office, garaged the car again, and went up to 2619. There was no one there, and no memos. I went straight on into 2618.

Roy, Leon Temple, and Janet Clark were there.

"Any luck?" Roy asked me.

"I don't know," I said.

"Well, we're starting to get some reports." Roy nodded with interest toward the cross-reference chart laid out on a big blackboard covering half of one wall. "Ed Orlin phoned a while ago. He located Gil's with no trouble and definitely placed the man and the woman there. Interesting stuff. I think we're getting somewhere."

"Fine," I said.

I went over to the board, topped with the caption: *X.*

In the column headed: "Names, Aliases," I read: *George Chester?*

Under "Appearance" it said: *Brown-haired, clean-cut, average height and build.*

I thought, thank you, Ed.

"Frequents": *Antique shops, Van Barth, Gil's. At one time frequented Gil's almost nightly.*

It was true, I had.

"Background": *Advertising? Newspapers? Formerly operated an upstate tavern-resort.*

Too close.

"Habits": *Collects pictures.*

"Character": *Eccentric, impractical. A pronounced drunk.*

This last heading was something that had been added by Roy in the Isleman and Sandler jobs. He imagined he had invented it, and valued it accordingly.

I said, standing beside the word-portrait of myself: "We seem to be getting somewhere."

"That isn't all," Roy told me. "Leon and Janet have just returned from the Van Barth with more. We were discussing it, before putting it on the board."

He looked at Leon, and Leon gave his information in neat, precise, third-person language.

"That's right," he said. "First of all it was established that Chester was in the lounge on Saturday night. He did not check the Judas picture he bought, but he was overheard talking about it with the woman accompanying him. And the woman with him was Pauline Delos."

I registered surprise.

"Are you sure?"

"No doubt about it, George. She was recognized by the waiter, the bartender, and the checkroom girl, from the pictures of her published in today's papers. Delos was in there Saturday night, with a man answering to the description on the board, and they were talking about a picture called *Judas* something-or-other. There can be no doubt about it." He looked at me for a long moment, in which I said nothing, then he finally asked: "I feel that's significant, don't you? Doesn't this alter the whole character of the assignment we are on? Personally, I think it does. Somebody raised the very same question this morning, and now it looks as though he had been right."

I said: "That's logical. Do the police know Delos was in there Saturday night?"

"Of course. Everyone in the place promptly told them."

"Do the police know we are looking for the man with her?"

"No. But they are certainly looking for him, now. We didn't say anything, because we thought this was exclusive with us. But what should we do about it? We're looking for George Chester, and yet this Delos tie-up is terrific, seems to me."

I nodded, and lifted Roy's phone.

"Right," I said. When I had Steve Hagen I barked into the receiver: "Steve? Listen. The woman with our man was Pauline Delos."

The other end of the wire went dead for five, ten, fifteen, twenty seconds.

"Hello, Steve? Are you there? This is George Stroud. We have discovered that the woman who was with the person we want was Pauline Delos. Does this mean something?"

I looked at Roy, Janet, and Leon. They seemed merely expectant, with no second thoughts apparent in their faces. At the other end of the wire I heard what I thought was a faint sigh from Steve Hagen.

"Nothing in particular," he said, carefully. "I knew that she saw this go-between. Perhaps I should have told you. But the fact that she was with him that night does not concern the matter we have in hand. What we want, and what we've got to have, is the name and whereabouts of the man himself. Delos is a blind alley, as far as our investigation is concerned. The murder is one story. This is a different, unrelated one. Is that plain?"

I said I understood him perfectly, and after I broke the

connection I repeated the explanation almost verbatim to the three people in the room.

Roy was complacent.

"Yes," he said. "But I said all along this was an issue related to some recent crisis, and now we know damn well it is."

He rose and went over to the blackboard, picked up some chalk. I watched him as he wrote under "Associates": *Pauline Delos*. Where the line crossed "Antique shops," "Gil's," "Van Barth" he repeated the name. Then he began to add a new column.

"At the same time, Leon and Janet brought in something more tangible," he went on. "Tell George about it."

Leon's small and measured voice resumed the report. "When they left the cocktail lounge of the Van Barth, our subject forgot something and left it behind him."

Nothing about me moved except my lips.

"Yes?"

Leon nodded toward Roy's desk and his eyes indicated an envelope. I seemed to float toward it, wondering whether this had all been an extravagant, cold-blooded farce they had put together with Hagen, whether I had actually mislaid or forgotten something that gave me away altogether. But the envelope was blank.

"A handkerchief," I heard Leon say, as from a great distance. "It can probably be traced, because it's obviously expensive, and it has what I believe is an old laundry mark."

Of course. She had borrowed it. When she spilled her cocktail I had used it, then given it to her. And it had been left there.

I turned the envelope over and shook the handkerchief from the unsealed flap. Yes. I could even see, faintly, the old stain.

"I wouldn't touch it, George," said Leon. "We may be able to raise a few fingerprints. It's a very fine, smooth fabric."

So I had to do that. I picked up the handkerchief and unfolded it. And laid it down and spread it out, very carefully and cautiously.

"I imagine it already has plenty," I said. "The waitress's, the cashier's, yours, one more set won't matter." I inspected the familiar square of linen with grave attention. It was one of a lot I had bought at Blanton's & Dent's, about a year ago. And there was the faint, blurred, but recoverable laundry mark on a bit of the hem, several months old, for it must have been put there when I last spent a week in the city and sent some of my things to a midtown laundry. "Yes, I imagine this can be traced."

I refolded the handkerchief, stuffed it back into the envelope. I could now account for the presence of my own fingerprints, but I knew I could not save the handkerchief itself from the mill.

I handed the envelope to Leon.

"Do you want to take this to Sacher & Roberts?" That was the big commercial laboratory we used for such work. "Whatever they find, we'll put another team on it. I suppose Dick and Louella relieved you at the Van Barth?"

"Oh, sure. Our man comes in there once or twice a week, they said."

"We've got the fellow covered at this place called Gil's, and at the Van Barth," Roy pointed out. "He'll come back, and then we've got him."

I nodded, rather thoughtfully. I said: "Certainly. He'll return to one place or the other. Then that will be that."

I don't know how that conference broke up. I think Leon went on to Sacher & Roberts. I believe I left Roy making additional entries on the big progress-board. I told him to eat and get some rest when he'd finished, I would be leaving around seven.

If they actually brought out prints on that handkerchief, we would all have to volunteer our own, mine with the rest. That in itself I had taken care of. But for a long, long time in my own office I sat trying to remember whether my fingerprints could be found anywhere on Pauline's overnight bag. Such a duplication could not be explained away. Hardly.

I forced myself to relive that last day with Pauline. No. I had not touched that grip anywhere except on the handle, and Pauline's final touches had certainly smudged them all out.

Sometime in the afternoon I took a call from Don Klausmeyer.

"Oh, yes, Don," I said. "Any luck with Patterson?"

Don's slow, malicious, pedantic voice told me: "I had a little trouble, but I found her. I've been talking to her for about an hour, going over old catalogues of her shows, looking at her fifth-rate pictures, and trying to keep her four kids out of my hair."

"Okay. Shoot."

"I have turned up one very significant fact. Louise Patterson was the customer who bid, unsuccessfully, for her own picture in the dealer's shop that night. A friend saw her canvas there, told her about it, and it was Patterson's hope that she could buy it back for herself. God knows why."

"I see. Anything else?"

"Do you understand? It was Patterson herself, in the shop that night."

"I get it. And?"

"And she described the man who bought the picture, at great length. Are you ready to take it?"

"Let's have it."

"This is Patterson speaking. Quote. He was a smug, self-satisfied, smart-alecky bastard just like ten million other rubber-stamp sub-executives. He had brown hair, brown eyes, high cheekbones, symmetrical and lean features. His face looked as though he scrubbed and shaved it five times a day. He weighed between one sixty and one sixty-five. Gray tweed suit, dark blue hat and necktie. He knows pictures, says she, and is certainly familiar with the works of L. Patterson, which he doubtless collects, but only for their snob-appeal. Personally, I think the dame overestimates herself. She admits she's been forgotten for the last ten years. But to go on. Our man is a good deal of an exhibitionist. He imagines he is Superman and that is what he plays at being. The woman with him was beautiful if you like Lesbians in standard, Park Avenue models. Unquote. Got it?"

"Yes."

"Does it help?"

"Some," I said.

"I've been poking around the studio-loft she lives in— God what a paradise for rats and termites—looking at acres and acres of pictures. Artistically she's impossible." How would Don know? "But they reminded me of something I'm sure I've seen somewhere very recently. If I can only remember what it is, maybe I'll have another lead."

He laughed and I echoed him, but I was staring straight at *Study in Fury* on the wall opposite me.

"Maybe you will, but don't worry about it. I'll see you tomorrow."

When he hung up I stared at that picture, without really

seeing it, for a long five minutes. Then I took my scribbled notes and went into Roy's empty office and duly entered Don's report on the chart. By now it was crystallizing into a very unpleasant definition of myself indeed. And after that, I took three good, recent photographs of Earl Janoth out of the morgue.

A little past seven o'clock Roy returned. We arranged about relieving each other on the following day and then I went out, feeling I'd had about all I could stand for the time being. But I still had work to do.

At the cabstand I had that afternoon selected as the likeliest, I got my first real break. A good one. A driver identified Janoth as a passenger he'd ridden a little after ten o'clock last Saturday night. The driver was positive. He knew when he'd picked him up, and where, and where he'd put him down. A block from Hagen's.

I knew this might save my neck, as a last desperate resort. But it would not necessarily save my home.

It was around midnight when I reached Marble Road. Georgia and Georgette were asleep.

I found *The Temptation of St. Judas* where I had left it, in a closet downstairs, and in twenty minutes I had it concealed in back of another canvas.

It could be discovered, and easily, if they ever really caught up with me. But if anyone ever got this far, I was finished anyway.

EARL JANOTH III

FIVE days after Steve first organized the search we had enough material concerning that damned phantom to write a long biography of him. We had dates, addresses, his background, a complete verbal description of him, X-rays of every last thought, emotion, and impulse he'd ever had. I knew that blundering weak fool better than his own mother. If I shut my eyes I could actually see him standing in front of me, an imbecilic wisp of a smile on his too good-looking face, I could hear his smooth, studied, disarming voice uttering those round, banal whimsicalities he apparently loved, I could almost reach out and touch him, this horrid wraith who had stumbled into my life from nowhere to bring about Pauline's death and my possible ruin.

Yet we didn't have the man himself. We had nothing.

"Candidly, I think you are holding something back," said George Stroud. He was talking to Steve. I had insisted on being present, though not directly participating, when we re-examined the paralysis that seemed to grip our plans. "And I think that thing, whatever it may be, is the one solid fact we need to wrap up the whole business."

"Stick to the facts," said Steve. "Your imagination is running away with you."

"I think not."

We were in Steve's office, Steve behind his desk, myself a little to one side of it, Stroud facing Steve. The room was filled with sunlight, but to me it looked dim, like the bottom of a pool of water. I don't believe I'd slept more than two hours a night in the last week.

The damned wolves were closing in on me. I'd been questioned by dozens of detectives and members of the district attorney's staff three, four, and sometimes five times a day, every day. At first they'd been polite. Now they weren't bothering much with that any more.

And Wayne knew it. Carr knew it. They all knew it. It was a secret only to the general public. In the downtown district and on Forty-second Street it was open knowledge. Nobody, conspicuously, had phoned or come near me for days. The more tightly the official gang closed in on me, the farther my own crowd drew away. The more they isolated me, the easier it became for the police. I could handle one pack of wolves, but not two.

There was no real evidence against me. Not yet. But neither was there any prospect that the pressure to get it would be relaxed.

I could stand that. But we had to find that damned will-o'-the-wisp, and find him before anyone else did. He was the one serious threat I faced. If the police got to him first, as at any moment they might, and eventually would, I knew exactly what he would say, and what would happen.

It didn't make sense. We had this mountain of data, and yet we were, for all practical purposes, right where we had started.

"All right, let's stick to the facts," Stroud told Steve. "You say this man is the key figure in a political-industrial deal. But we haven't turned up one single political connection, and no business connections worth mentioning. Why not? I say, because there aren't any."

Steve told him sharply: "There are. You simply haven't dug deeply enough to get them. I'm holding nothing back except rumors and suspicions. They'd do you no good at all. In fact, they'd simply throw you off."

Stroud's voice was soft and rather pleasant, but it carried a lot of emphasis.

"I couldn't be thrown off more than I was, when you knew Delos was right in the middle of the situation, but you somehow forgot to tell me so."

This senseless bickering would get us nowhere. I had to intervene.

"What is your own opinion, George?" I asked him. "How do you account for the fact we seem to be going around in circles? It isn't like you to be held up so long on a simple thing like this. What is your honest theory about this business?"

Stroud turned and gave me a long, keen regard. He was what I had always classified as one of those hyper-perceptive people, not good at action but fine at pure logic and theory. He was the sort who could solve a bridge-hand at a glance, down to the last play, but in a simple business deal he would be helpless. The cold fighter's and gambler's nerve that Steve had was completely lacking in him, and he would consider it something foreign or inhuman, if indeed he understood it at all.

After five days of the present job Stroud showed the strain. That was a good thing, because he had to understand this was not merely a routine story.

"Yes, I have a theory," he told me. "I believe the Delos murder and the man we want are so closely connected they are identical. I am forced to reject Steve's idea that one is only accidentally related to the other."

I nodded. It was inevitable, of course. We hadn't selected Stroud to lead the investigation because of his good looks, fancy imagination, or vanity, which was colossal.

I glanced at Steve, trusting he would go on from there more sensibly.

"I follow your reasoning, George," he said. "And I think you are right. But here is something you've overlooked, and we now have to consider. We know that Pauline had knowledge of this big combination. She helped to fill in the background, fragmentary as it is, of the whole thing. She would naturally follow it up if she could. Suppose she did just that? Suppose somebody caught her doing it? And got to her first. Have you thought of that?"

Stroud paused, remote and deliberate. He was just a little too keen for this.

"If this deal is for such high stakes, and if the other parties have already gone the limit," he said, and stopped for an even longer pause, "then we're in rough company. Our man is either in Mexico and still going south, or he has already been disposed of altogether, in such a way he will never again be found."

"That can't be," Steve told him, sharply. "Here's why. A man like this, eccentric, with a wide and varied circle of acquaintances, married and with at least one child, a responsible position somewhere, would leave a pretty big hole if he suddenly dropped out of circulation. Yet you've been in close touch with the Missing Persons Bureau—since when?"

"Tuesday morning."

"Tuesday. And no one like our man has been reported. His disappearance would certainly leak out somewhere, somehow. It hasn't, and that means he's still around." Stroud nodded, cautiously, and Steve went swiftly to another point. "Now let's look at some of these other leads a little more closely. You're still checking the list of upstate liquor licenses suspended or not renewed with the Board?"

Stroud passed a handkerchief across his perspiring face.

"Yes, but that's a tall order. There are hundreds." Stroud looked down for a moment of abstraction at the handkerchief, then he folded the cloth with great deliberation and thrust it slowly and carefully away. "The list is being fed straight to me. If I get anything, you'll know at once."

It was a strange thing to say. Of course we would.

"You've seen the story *Newsways* ran about this Patterson woman?" Steve asked, and Stroud said he had. "It's too early for results. But our spread is going to put that woman on the map. Somebody is certain to recognize and remember that *Judas* picture from our description of it. Our evaluation of it as 'priceless' is sure to locate it. It's my hunch the picture alone will nail our man to the wall."

Stroud smiled faintly, but said nothing, and then they went on to other lines of investigation involving tax lists, advertising agencies, newspapers, fingerprints on a handkerchief, all of them ending in so much fog and vapor. At length, I heard Steve saying: "Now those bars, art galleries, and so on."

"All covered."

"Exactly. And why hasn't our man shown, by now? To me, that's fantastic. No one suddenly abandons his habitual routine of life. Not without some good reason."

"I've already suggested he has either left the country, or been killed," said Stroud. "Here are some more versions of the same general theory. He may have killed Delos, himself, and in that case he's naturally not making himself conspicuous. Or he knows that he's in fast company, knows the score, and he's gone to ground, right where he is, so that the same thing won't happen to him."

I carefully looked away from Steve, and also away from Stroud. In a curious way Stroud's conclusion was almost perfect. The room was momentarily too quiet.

"You think he may believe himself to be in danger?" Steve presently asked.

"He knows somebody is playing for keeps. Why wouldn't he be worried?"

"And he's keeping pretty well under cover." Steve appeared to be groping toward something. He stared absently at Stroud. "At least, he stays away from all the places where he always went before." Steve was silent for a moment, then he asked: "How many people in the organization, George, know about this particular job?"

Stroud seemed not to understand him.

"Our own?"

"Right here at Janoth Enterprises. How many, at a guess?"

Stroud displayed a thin smile. "Well, with fifty-three people now working on this assignment, I'd say everyone knows about it. The entire two thousand."

"Yes," Steve admitted. "I guess so."

"Why?"

"Nothing. For a second I thought I had something." Steve came back into himself, leaned aggressively forward. "All right, I guess that reports on everything. And it's still nothing."

"Do you think I've missed a bet anywhere?" Stroud demanded.

"Just bear down on it, that's all."

"I shall. Now that we've decided the killing and our particular baby are identical twins, there are a lot more lines we can follow."

"What lines?"

Stroud got up to go. He put a cigarette in his mouth, reflected before lighting it.

"For one thing, I'll have some men cover all the cab-stands in the neighborhood of Pauline Delos' apartment. On the night of her death, and a few minutes after it, somebody took a taxi away from that vicinity, and he couldn't help being rather noticeable." He lit his cigarette, drew deeply, casually exhaled. "The driver will remember, and tell us all about him."

My eyes went to Steve, and stayed there. I knew he understood, because he did not, even for a second, glance in my direction.

"I don't follow that, George," he said, in a dead-level voice.

"It's quite simple. Our subject took Pauline to Gil's, to a number of antique shops, and to the Van Barth. Why wouldn't he take her home? Of course he did. Our timing checks with the police timing. He took her home and then he had to leave. No matter what happened there, no matter who killed her, no matter what he saw or what he knew, he had to leave. The first and most obvious line to follow is that he left in a taxi."

I was forced to say, "Perhaps he had his own car."

"Perhaps he did."

"He may have walked," said Steve. "Or taken a bus."

"That's true. But we can't afford to pass up the fact he may have done none of those things. He may have taken a cab. We'll just put a bet on that and hope for the best." Stroud had never lacked confidence in himself, and now it was engraved all over him. He moved toward the door. Standing there, he added, finally: "It's my hunch we'll discover he did take a cab, we'll locate the driver, find out where he went, and that will close our whole assignment."

There was a long and complete silence after he had gone, with Steve intently staring at the door that closed behind him. I thought I was reading his mind. "Yes. You're right."

"About what?"

"We'll close the assignment, all right. We're going to call the whole job off."

"No, we're not. Why should we? I was thinking of something else. About Stroud. I don't like that bastard."

"It's the same thing. I don't want Stroud looking for that taxi."

There was a smoldering anger in Steve that seemed to feed itself, perceptibly mounting.

"That's nothing. You'll never be tied to that. Our staff is good, but not that good. What worries me is what's holding us up? Why is it the only smart idea Stroud can dream up is one we don't like? He's cutting corners somewhere—but where?"

"Pull him off the job. Right now. Before he sends another team out looking for that driver. I hate the way his mind works."

Steve's eyes were shining like an animal's, and as insensate. "We can't drop the inquiry, and there's no point in replacing Stroud. We have to go through with it, and Stroud has to deliver the goods. He has to do it a damn sight quicker, that's all. We started with an inside track, but that advantage we're losing, now, every hour."

I thought of hunters stalking big game, and while they did so, the game closed in on its own prey, and with the circle eventually completing itself, unknown disaster drew near to the hunters. It was a thing ordained. I said: "You don't know the whole situation. There have been a number of informal, really secret board meetings recently, and that dinner last Saturday—"

Steve interrupted, still watching me. "Yes. You told me."

"Well, if this business goes the wrong way, or even drags itself out, that's all they'll need to take some kind of overt action. I'm certain they've been discussing it these last four or five days. If that should happen—well, that's even worse than this."

Steve seemed not to hear. He looked out at me, and upon the whole of life, deeply and steadily as a bronze, inhumanized idol. Surprisingly, he asked: "You haven't been sleeping much, have you?"

"Not since it happened."

He nodded, spoke with persuasive but impersonal finality. "You're going to a hospital. You've got a strep throat. Forget about everything. Doc Reiner is sending you to bed for a couple of days. With no visitors. Except me."

GEORGETTE STROUD

I HADN'T seen George when he came home last night. He had worked late, even though it had been Sunday. For that matter, I hadn't seen him any evening during the past week. It was nothing unusual for him to work late, either here or at the office. Some evenings he did not return at all.

But this Monday morning I knew something was different. It was not just another long and tough assignment, though that is what he said it was.

When he came down to breakfast I saw what I had only been feeling, but without knowing it. Now I knew something was altogether unusual, and I forced myself to search for it.

He kissed Georgia and myself and sat down. Always, when he started breakfast, he said something about the first dish he happened to see. Now he began with his grapefruit, and said nothing.

"Tell me a story, George," Georgia presently demanded, as though a perfectly novel idea had just occurred to her.

"Story? Story? What's a story, anyway? Never heard of it."

That was all right, though a little mechanical.

"Go on. George said you would. She promised."

"All right, I'll tell you a story. It's about a little girl named Sophia."

"How old?"

"Six."

Again there was that wrong note. She always had to coax him before he gave her right age.

"So what did she do?"

"Well, this is really about Sophia and her very best friend, another little girl."

"And what was her name?"

"Sonia, as it happens."

"How old?"

"Six."

"So what did they do?"

I saw, for the first time, he must have lost a lot of weight. And when he talked to me, he was not there at all. Normally, he wrapped himself in clouds of confetti, but anyone who knew him at all understood exactly what he meant and just where he could be found. But now he really, really wasn't there. His light evasions weren't light. They were actual evasions. The clouds of confetti were steel doors.

It crossed my mind he had been like this two years ago, during the affair I knew he had with Elizabeth Stoltz. That one I was certain about. And there had been others before that, I had believed then, and more than ever believed now.

A wave of utter unreality swept over me. And I recognized the mood, too well, like the first twinges of a recurrent ailment. It was too hideous to be real. That, that was what made it finally so hideous.

"Well, Sophia never saw her friend Sonia except at certain times. Only when Sophia climbed up on a chair and looked into the mirror to wash her face or comb her hair. Whenever she did that she always found Sonia, of all people, there ahead of her."

"So what did they do then?"

"So then they had long, long talks. 'What's the idea, always getting in my way?' Sophia would ask. 'You go away from here, Sonia, and leave me alone.' "

"So what did Sonia say?"

"Well, that's the strangest thing of all. Sonia never said a word. Not one word. But whatever Sophia did in front of the looking glass, Sonia copied her. Even when Sophia stuck out her tongue and called Sonia an old copycat."

"Then what happened?"

"This went on for a long time, and Sophia was pretty mad, believe me." Yes, George, Sophia was pretty damn mad. Just how many years, George, did it go on? "But she thought it over, and one day she told Sonia, 'If you don't stop getting in my way every time I come to the mirror, Sonia, why, I'll never get out of your way, either.' "

"So then what?"

"That's just what Sophia did. Every time Sonia, the little girl who never talked, came to the mirror to comb her hair, so did Sophia. And everything Sonia did, Sophia copied her right back."

No. I don't think so. I think they both did something else. They simply went away from each other.

It can't be. I can't go through that horror again.

What is the matter with him? Is he insane? I can't fall over that terrible cliff again.

Can he ever change and grow up? He's been all right since the Stoltz girl. I thought that would be the last, because she had to be the last. There is a limit beyond which nerves cannot be bruised and torn, and still live. If that is what it is, I cannot endure it again.

Is he quite sane? He can't be, to be so blind.

"I have a best friend," Georgia announced.

"I should hope so."

"A new one."

"What do you and your best friend do?"

"We play games. But sometimes she steals my crayons. Her name's Pauline."

"I see. And then what happens?"

It was too pat, like something rehearsed and coming out of a machine, a radio or a phonograph.

The horn of the school bus sounded and Georgia jumped up. I dabbed at her face with my napkin, then followed her into the hall where she rushed for her school bag, contents one drawing pad, one picture book, and the last time I looked into it, a handful of loose beads, some forgotten peanuts, the broken top of a fountain pen.

I stood there for a moment after I kissed her good-bye and she ran down the walk. Perhaps I was wrong.

I had to be wrong. I would be wrong. Until I was forced to be otherwise.

On my way back to the breakfast room I saw the last issue of *Newsways*, and remembered something. I brought it with me.

"George," I said, "you forgot to bring home a *Newsways*."

He went on with his eggs and coffee and said, absently: "It slipped my mind. I'll bring one home tonight without fail. And *Personalities*, just off."

"Never mind the *Newsways*, I bought one yesterday." He looked at me and saw the magazine, and for just an instant there was something strange and drawn in his face I had never seen before, then it was gone so quickly I wasn't sure it had been there at all. "There's something in it I meant to ask you about. Did you read the article about Louise Patterson?"

"Yes, I read it."

"It's grand, isn't it? It's just what you've been saying

for years." I quoted a sentence from the article. " 'Homunculus grows to monstrous size, with all the force of a major explosion, by grace of a new talent suddenly shooting meteorlike across the otherwise turgid skies of the contemporary art world. Louise Patterson may view her models through a microscope, but the brush she wields is Gargantuan.' "

"Yes, it's grand. But it is not what I've been saying for years."

"Anyway, they recognize her talent. Don't be so critical, just because they use different words than you would. At least they admit she's a great painter, don't they?"

"That they do."

Something was away off key. The words were meant to be lightly skeptical, but the tone of his voice was simply flat.

"For heaven's sake, George, don't pretend you aren't pleased. You must have seven or eight Pattersons, and now they're all terribly valuable."

"Priceless. I believe that's the *Newsways* term for them." He dropped his napkin and stood up. "I'll have to run. I think I'll drive in as usual, unless you need the car."

"No, of course not. But wait, George. Here's one thing more." I found another paragraph in the same article, and read from it. " 'This week interest of the art world centered in the whereabouts of Patterson's lost masterpiece, her famed *Judas*, admittedly the most highly prized canvas of all among the priceless works that have come from the studio of this artist. Depicting two huge hands exchanging a coin, a consummate study in flaming yellow, red, and tawny brown, this composition was widely known some years ago, then it quietly dropped from view.' And so on."

I looked up from the magazine. George said: "Neat but

not gaudy. They make it sound like a rainbow at mid-night."

"That's not what I'm driving at. Would you know anything about that picture?"

"Why should I?"

"Didn't I see an unframed picture you brought home, about a week ago, something like that?"

"You sure did, Georgie-porgie. A copy of it."

"Oh, well. What became of it?"

George winked at me, but there was nothing warm in back of it. There was nothing at all. Just something blank.

"Took it to the office, of course. Where do you think those plumbers got such an accurate description of the original?" He patted my shoulder and gave me a quick kiss. "I'll have to step on it. I'll call you this afternoon."

When he'd gone, and I heard the car go down the driveway, I put down the magazine and slowly got up. I went out to Nellie in the kitchen, knowing how it feels to be old, really old.

EMORY MAFFERSON

I'D NEVER known Stroud very well until recently, and for that matter I didn't know him now. Consequently, I couldn't guess how, or whether, he fitted the Janoth pattern.

When he told me not to be the *Crimeways* type, that meant nothing. This was standard counsel on all of our publications, and for all I knew, Stroud was merely another of the many keen, self-centered, ambitious people in the organization who moved from office to office, from alliance to alliance, from one ethical or political fashion to another, never with any real interest in life except to get more money next year than this, and always more than his colleagues did.

Yet I had a feeling Stroud was not that simple. All I knew about him, in fact, was that he considered himself pretty smooth, seemed to value his own wit, and never bought anything we manufactured here.

Neither did I. Until now.

Leon Temple was in Stroud's office when I came in late that Monday morning, asking Stroud to O.K. an order for some money he swore he had to have for this new, hysterical assignment nearly everyone except myself seemed to be working on. From what I gathered, Temple did nothing but loaf around the cocktail lounge of the Van Barth with a nice little wisp of a thing by the name of Janet Clark. Roaming around the office and trying to figure the best approach to Stroud, I felt like an outsider. They were having one long, happy party, while I spent my days in the ancient Homicide Bureau or the crumbling ruins of the District Attorney's office.

When Stroud signed the order for cash and Leon Temple had gone, I went over and lifted myself to the window ledge in back of his desk. He swung his chair around and in the cross-light I saw what I had not noticed before, that the man's face was lined and hard.

"Anything new, Emory?" he asked.

"Well. Yes. Largely routine stuff. But I wanted to talk about something else."

"Shoot."

"Do you know about the strange thing that happened a week ago last Saturday night?"

"The night of the murder?"

"Yes. But this is about Funded Individuals. I met Fred Steichel, M.E. of Jennett-Donohue, that night Do you know him?"

"I've met him. But I don't know what you are referring to."

"Well, I know Fred pretty well. His wife and mine were classmates, and still see a lot of each other. We met at a dinner, and there was quite a party afterwards. Fred got drunk, and he began to tell me all about Funded Individuals. In fact, he knew as much about it as I did."

Stroud showed no great concern. "No reason why he shouldn't. It isn't a profound secret. Anything like that gets around."

"Sure, in a general way. But this was different. Fred's all right when he's sober, but he's obnoxious when he's drunk, and that night he was deliberately trying to make himself about as unpleasant as possible. It amused him to recite our computations, quote the conclusions we'd reached, and even repeat some of the angles we'd tried out for a while and then abandoned. The point is, he had the exact figures, the precise steps we'd taken, and he had, for instance, a lot of the phrases I'd personally used in my reports. Not just generally correct, but absolutely verbatim. In other words, there was a leak somewhere, and he'd seen the actual research, the reports, and the findings."

"And then?"

"Well, I got pretty sore. It's one thing that Jennett-Donohue hears rumors about what we're doing, but it's another thing if they have access to supposedly confidential records. I mean, what the hell? I just didn't like the way Fred talked about Funded Individuals. As though it's a dead pigeon. According to him, I was wasting my time. It was only a matter of weeks or days before the whole scheme would be shelved. So the more I thought it over, the less I liked it. He didn't get that data just by accident, and his cockiness wasn't based entirely on a few drinks."

Stroud nodded.

"I see. And you thought it's something we ought to know about."

"I did, and I do. I don't pretend to understand it, but it's my baby, I invested a lot of work in it, and it's something more than the run-of-the-mill mirages we put together around here. It fascinates me. There's something about it almost real." Stroud was at least listening with interest, if not agreement, and I pressed the argument. "It's not just another inspirational arrow shot into the air. This is a cash-and-carry business. And the minute you know there can be a society in which every individual has an actual monetary value of one million dollars, and he's returning dividends on himself, you also know that nobody is going to shoot, starve, or ruin that perfectly sound investment."

Stroud gave me a faint, understanding, but wintry smile.

"I know," he said. "All right, I'll tell Hagen or Earl about this peculiar seepage of our confidential material."

"But that's the point, I already did. That was the strange thing about that Saturday night. I phoned you first, and I couldn't reach you, then I phoned Hagen. He was in, and he agreed with me that it was damn important. He said he would take it up with Earl, and he wanted to see me the first thing Monday morning. Then I didn't hear another word from him."

Stroud leaned back in his chair, studying me, and plainly puzzled. "You called Hagen that night?"

"I had to let somebody know."

"Of course. What time did you call?"

"Almost immediately. I told Steichel I would, and the bastard just laughed."

"Yes, but what time?"

"Well, about ten-thirty. Why?"

"And you talked only to Hagen? You didn't talk to Earl, did you?"

"I didn't talk to him, no. But he must have been there at the time I called. That's where he was that night, you know."

Stroud looked away from me, frowning.

"Yes, I know," he said, in a very tired, distant voice. "But exactly what did Hagen say, do you recall?"

"Not exactly. He told me he would take it up with Earl. That's a double-check on Earl's whereabouts, isn't it? And Hagen said he would see me Monday morning. But on Monday morning I didn't hear from him, I haven't heard from him since, and I began to wonder what happened. I thought maybe he'd relayed the whole matter to you."

"No, I'm sorry, he didn't. But I'll follow it up, of course. I quite agree with you, it's important. And with Hagen." I saw again that wintry smile, this time subzero. "A human life valued at a million paper dollars would make something of a story, wouldn't it? Don't worry, Emory, your dream-child will not be lost."

He was one of those magnetic bastards I have always admired and liked, and of course envied and hated, and I found myself, stupidly, believing him. I knew it couldn't be true, but I actually believed he was genuinely interested in protecting Funded Individuals, and would find a way, somehow, to give it a full hearing and then, in the end, contrive for it a big, actual trial. I smiled, digging some notes out of my pocket, and said: "Well, that's all I wanted to talk about. Now, here's the latest dope the cops have on the Delos murder. I already told you they know she was out of town from late Friday until the following Saturday afternoon." Stroud gave a half nod, and concentrated his attention. I went on: "Yesterday they found out where she was. She was in Albany, with a man. There was a book of matches found in her apartment, from a night club in Albany that doesn't circulate its matches from coast to coast, only there on the spot, and in the course of a routine check-up with Albany hotels, they found that's where she actually was. Got it?"

He nodded, briefly, waiting and remote and again hard. I said: "The cops know all about this job you're doing here, by the way, and they're convinced the man you are looking for and the man who was with Delos last Friday and Saturday in Albany is one and the same person. Does that help or hinder you any?"

He said: "Go on."

"That's about all. They are sending a man up there this afternoon or tomorrow morning, with a lot of photographs which he will check with the night club, the hotel, and elsewhere. I told you they had the Delos woman's address book. Well, this morning they let me look at it. They've been rounding up pictures of every man mentioned on this extensive list of hers, and most likely the guy that was with her in Albany is one of them. Do you follow me?"

"I follow you."

"They know from the general description of this man, as they got it over the phone from the personnel of the hotel and the club up there, that he most definitely was not Janoth. At the hotel, they were registered as Mr. and Mrs. Andrew Phelps-Guyon, a phoney if there ever was one. Does the name mean anything to you?"

"No."

"Your name was in the woman's address book, by the way."

"Yes," he said. "I knew Pauline Delos."

"Well, that's all."

Stroud seemed to be considering the information I had given him.

"That's fine, Emory," he said, and flashed me a quick, heatless smile. "By the way, is the department looking for a photograph of me?"

"No. They've already got one. Something you once turned in for a license or a passport. The man they are sending upstate has quite a collection. He has fifty or sixty photographs."

"I see."

"I can go along to Albany with this fellow, if you like," I said. "If he doesn't accomplish anything else, I imagine he'll be able to identify the man you've been hunting for, yourself."

"I'm sure he will," he said. "But don't bother. I think that can be done better right here."

GEORGE STROUD IX

THE TWO lines of investigation, the organization's and the official one, drew steadily together like invisible pincers. I could feel them closing.

I told myself it was just a tool, a vast machine, and the machine was blind. But I had not fully realized its crushing weight and power. That was insane. The machine cannot be challenged. It both creates and blots out, doing each with glacial impersonality. It measures people in the same way that it measures money, and the growth of trees, the life-span of mosquitoes and morals, the advance of time. And when the hour strikes, on the big clock, that is indeed the hour, the day, the correct time. When it says a man is right, he is right, and when it finds him wrong, he is through, with no appeal. It is as deaf as it is blind.

Of course, I had asked for this.

I returned to the office from a lunch I could not remember having tasted. It had been intended as an interlude to plan for new eventualities and new avenues of escape.

The Janoth Building, covering half of a block, looked into space with five hundred sightless eyes as I turned again, of my own free will, and delivered myself once more to its stone intestines. The interior of this giant God was spick-and-span, restfully lighted, filled with the continuous echo of many feet. A visitor would have thought it nice.

Waiting for me, on my desk, I found the list of non-renewed licenses for out-of-town taverns, for six years ago. I knew this was the one that would have my own name.

That would have to be taken care of later. Right now, I could do nothing but stuff it into the bottom drawer of my desk.

I went into Roy's room and asked him: "Starved?"

"Considerably, considerably."

"The St. Bernards have arrived." He slowly stood up, rolled down the sleeves of his shirt. "Sorry if I kept you waiting. Any developments?"

"Not that I know of, but Hagen wants to see you. Maybe I'd better postpone lunch until you've talked with him."

"All right. But I don't think I'll keep you waiting."

I went upstairs. These conferences had daily become longer, more frequent, and more bitter. It was cold comfort to have a clear understanding of the abyss that Hagen and Janoth, particularly Janoth, saw before them.

For the hundredth time I asked myself why Earl had done this thing. What could possibly have happened on that night, in that apartment? God, what a price to pay. But it had happened. And I recognized that I wasn't really thinking of Janoth, at all, but of myself.

When I stepped into Hagen's office he handed me a note, an envelope, and a photograph.

"This just came in," he said. "We're giving the picture a half-page cut in *Newsways*, with a follow-up story."

The note and the envelope were on the stationery of a Fifty-seventh Street gallery. The photograph, a good, clear 4 x 6, displayed one wall of a Louise Patterson exhibition, with five of her canvases clearly reproduced. The note, from the dealer, simply declared the photograph had been taken at a show nine years ago, and was, as far as known, the only authentic facsimile of the picture mentioned by *Newsways* as lost.

[146]

There could be no mistaking the two hands of my *Judas*. It was right in the middle. The dealer duly pointed out, however, that it's original proper title was simply: *Study in Fundamentals*.

The canvas at the extreme right, though I recognized none of the others, was the *Study in Fury* that hung on my wall downstairs.

"This seems to answer the description," I said.

"Beyond any doubt. When we run that, quoting the dealer, I'm certain we'll uncover the actual picture." Maybe. It was still concealed behind another canvas on Marble Road. But I knew that if Georgette saw the follow-up, and she would, my story of finding a copy of it would not hold. For the photograph would be reproduced as the only known authentic facsimile. "But I hope to God we have the whole thing cleaned up long before then." I tensed as he looked at the photograph again, certain he would recognize the *Fury*. But he didn't. He laid it down, regarded me with a stare made out of acid. "George, what in hell's wrong? This has drifted along more than a week."

"It took us three weeks to find Isleman," I said.

"We're not looking for a man missing several months. We're looking for somebody that vanished a week ago, leaving a trail a mile wide. Something's the matter. What is it?" But, without waiting for an answer, he discarded the question, and began to check off our current leads. "How about those lapsed licenses?"

I said they were still coming in, and I was cross-checking them as fast as they were received. Methodically, then, we went over all the ground we had covered before. By now it was hash. I'd done a good job making it so.

Before leaving I asked about Earl, and learned he was

out of the hospital, after two days. And that was all I learned.

I returned to my office about an hour after I had come upstairs. When I walked in I found Roy, Leon Temple, and Phil Best. It was apparent, the second I stepped into the room, there had been a break.

"We've got him," said Leon.

His small and usually colorless face was all lit up. I knew I would never breath again.

"Where is he?"

"Right here. He came into this building just a little while ago."

"Who is he?"

"We don't know yet. But we've got him." I waited, watching him, and he explained: "I slipped some cash to the staff of the Van Barth, let them know there'd be some more, and they've all been looking around this district in their free hours. One of the porters picked him up and followed him here."

I nodded, feeling as though I'd been kicked in the stomach.

"Nice work," I said. "Where is this porter now?"

"Downstairs. When he phoned me, I told him to watch the elevators and follow the guy if he came out. He hasn't. Now Phil's bringing over the antique dealer, Eddy is bringing a waitress from Gil's, and then we'll have all six banks of elevators completely covered. I've told the special cops what to do when our man tries to leave. They'll grab him and make him identify himself from his first birthday up to now."

"Yes," I said. "I guess that's that." It was as though they had treed an animal, and that, in fact, was just the case. I was the animal. I said: "That's smart stuff, Leon. You used your head."

"Dick and Mike are down on the main floor, helping the fellow from the Van Barth. In about two minutes we'll have every door and exit covered, too."

I suddenly reached for my coat, but didn't go through with it. I couldn't, now, it was too late. Instead, I pulled out some cigarettes, moved around in back of my desk and sat down.

"You're certain it's thé right man?" I asked.

But of course there was no question. I had been seen on my way back from lunch. And followed.

"The porter is positive."

"All right," I said. The phone rang and mechanically I answered it. It was Dick, reporting that they now had the elevators fully covered. In addition to the porter, a night bartender at the Van Barth, Gil's waitress, and the dealer had all arrived. "All right," I said again. "Stay with it. You know what to do."

Methodically, Phil Best explained, in his shrewish voice, what was unmistakably plain.

"If he doesn't come out during the afternoon, we're sure to pick him up at five-thirty, when the building empties." I nodded, but my stunned and scattered thoughts were beginning to pull themselves together. "It'll be jammed, as usual, but we can have every inch of the main floor covered."

"He's in the bag," I said. "We can't miss. I'm going to stay right here until we get him. I'll send out for supper, and if necessary I'll sleep upstairs in the restroom on the twenty-seventh floor. Personally, I'm not going to leave this office until we've got it all sewed up. How about the rest of you?"

I wasn't listening to what they replied.

Even Roy would know that if a man came into a building, and didn't go out, he must logically still be inside of it. And this inescapable conclusion must eventually be followed by one and only one logical course of action.

Sooner or later my staff must go through the building, floor by floor and office by office, looking for the only man in it who never went home.

It wouldn't take long, when they did that. The only question was, who would be the first to make the suggestion.

LOUISE PATTERSON

T HIS time when I answered the doorbell, which had been ringing steadily for the last four days, I found that tall, thin, romantic squirt, Mr. Klausmeyer, from that awful magazine. It was his third visit, but I didn't mind. He was such a polite, dignified worm, much stuffier than anyone I'd ever met before, he gave my apartment a crazy atmosphere of respectability or something.

"I hope I'm not disturbing you, Mrs. Patterson," he said, making the same mistake he'd made before.

"MISS Patterson," I shrieked, laughing. "You are, but come in. Haven't you caught your murderer yet?"

"We aren't looking for any murderer, Miss Patterson. I have told you the—"

"Save that for *Hokum Fact's* regular subscribers," I said. "Sit down."

He carefully circled around the four children, where the two younger ones, Pete's and Mike's, were helping the older pair, Ralph's, as they sawed and hammered away at some boards and boxes and wheels, building a wagon, or maybe it was some new kind of scooter. Mr. Klausmeyer carefully hitched up his pants, he would, before sitting down in the big leather chair that had once been a rocker.

"You have us confused with *True Facts*," he firmly corrected me. "That's another outfit altogether, not in the same field with any of our publications. I'm with Janoth Enterprises. Until recently I was on the staff of *Personalities*." With wonderful irony he added, "I'm sure you've heard of it. Perhaps you've even read it. But right now I'm working on a special—"

"I know, Mr. Klausmeyer. You wrote that article about me in *Newsways Bunk*." He looked so mad that if he hadn't come because of his job I'm sure he would have gotten up and gone like a bat out of hell. "Never mind," I said, simply whooping. "I enjoyed it, Mr. Klausmeyer. Really I did. And I appreciated it, too, even if you did get it all cockeyed, and I know you didn't really mean any of those nice things you tried to say about me. I know you're just looking for that murderer. Would you like some muscatel? It's all I have."

I dragged out what was left of a gallon of muscatel and found one of my few remaining good tumblers. It was almost clean.

"No, thank you," he said. "About that article, Miss Patterson—"

"Not even a little?"

"No, really. But regarding the article—"

"It isn't very good," I admitted. "I mean the wine," I explained, then I realized I was simply bellowing, and felt aghast. Mr. Klausmeyer hadn't done anything to me, he looked like the sensitive type who takes everything personally, and the least I could do was to refrain from insulting him. I made up my mind to act exactly like an artist should. I poured myself a glass of the muscatel and urged him, quite gently, "I do wish you'd join me."

"No, thanks. Miss Patterson, I didn't write that article in *Newsways*."

"Oh, you didn't?"

"No."

"Well, I thought it was a perfectly wonderful story." It came to me that I'd said the wrong thing again, and I simply howled. "I mean, within limits. Please, Mr. Klausmeyer, don't mind me. I'm not used to having my pictures labeled 'costly.' Or was it 'invaluable'? The one the murderer bought for fifty bucks."

Mr. Klausmeyer was mad, I could see, and probably I was boring him besides. I swore I would keep my mouth shut and act reasonably for at least fifteen minutes, no matter what he said, and no matter how I felt. Fifteen minutes. That's not so long.

"I merely supplied some of the information," Mr. Klausmeyer carefully explained. "For instance, I supplied the *Newsways* writer with the description of the *Judas* picture, exactly as you gave it to me."

The son of a bitch.

"God damn it all," I screamed, "where do you get that *Judas* stuff? I told you the name of the picture was *Study in Fundamentals*. What in hell do you mean by giving my own picture some fancy title I never thought of at all? How do you dare, you horrible little worm, how do you dare to throw your idiocy all over my work?"

I looked at him through a haze of rage. He was another picture burner. I could tell it just by looking at his white, stuffy face. Another one of those decent, respectable maniacs who'd like nothing better than to take a butcher knife and slash canvases, slop them with paint, burn them. By God, he looked exactly like Pete. No, Pete's way had been to use them to cover up broken window panes, plug up draughts, and stop leaks in the ceiling. He was more the official type. His method would be to bury them in an authorized warehouse somewhere, destroy the records, and let them stay there forever.

I drank off the muscatel, poured myself some more, and tried to listen to him.

"I did use your own title, I assure you, but there must have been a slip somewhere in the writing and editing. That will be corrected in a story *Newsways* is now running, with a photograph of the *Study in Fundamentals*."

"I know you, you damned arsonist." His large gray eyes bugged out just the way Ralph's had when he showed me the pile of scraps and ashes and charred fragments, all that was left of five years' work, heaped up in the fireplace. How proud he'd been. You really amount to something, I guess, if you know how to destroy something new and creative. "What do you want now?" I demanded. "Why do you come here?"

I saw that Mr. Klausmeyer was quite pale. I guess if he hadn't been a tame caterpillar doing an errand for *Anything But the News* he would have picked up Elroy's scout hatchet and taken a swing at me.

"We've located the man who bought your picture, Miss Patterson," he said, with great control. "We believe we know where he is, and he'll be found at any moment. We wish you'd come to the office, so that you can identify him. Of course, we'll pay you for your time and trouble. We'll give you a hundred dollars if you can help us. Will you?"

"So you've found the murderer," I said.

With emphatic weariness, Mr. Klausmeyer repeated: "We are not looking for a murderer, Miss Patterson. I assure you, we want this man in some altogether different connection."

"Crap," I said.

"I beg your pardon?"

"Nonsense. Detectives have been around here, asking me the same questions you have. You are both looking for the same man, the one who bought my picture, and murdered that Delos woman. What do you think I am? Apparently you think I'm a complete dope."

"No," Mr. Klausmeyer told me, strongly. "Anything but that. Will you come back to the office with me?"

A hundred dollars was a hundred dollars.

"I don't know why I should help to catch a man with brains enough to like my *Study in Fundamentals*. I haven't got so many admirers I can afford to let any of them go to the electric chair."

Mr. Klausmeyer's face showed that he fully agreed, and it pained him that he couldn't say so.

"But perhaps we can help you reclaim your picture. You wanted to buy it back, didn't you?"

"No. I didn't want to buy it back, I just didn't want it to rot in that black hole of Calcutta."

And I knew no one would ever see that picture again. It was already at the bottom of the East River. The murderer would have to do away with it to save his own hide. He would get rid of anything that connected him with the dead woman.

Yet one more noble little angel of destruction.

I realized this, feeling mad and yet somehow cold. It was no use telling myself that I didn't care. The canvas was not one of my best. And yet I did care. It was hard enough to paint the things, without trying to defend them afterwards from self-appointed censors and jealous lovers and microscopic deities. Like Mr. Klausmeyer.

"All right," I said. "I'll go. But only for the hundred dollars."

Mr. Klausmeyer rose like something popping out of a box. God, he was elegant. When he died they wouldn't have to embalm him. The fluid already ran in his veins.

"Certainly," he said, warmly.

I looked around and found my best hat on the top shelf of the bookcases. Edith, who was four—she was Mike's—scolded me for taking away her bird's nest. I explained the nest would be back in place before nightfall. Leaving, I put the whole trading-post in charge of Ralph junior until further notice. He looked up, and I think he even heard me. Anyway, he understood.

In a taxi, on the way to his office, Mr. Klausmeyer tried to be friendly.

"Splendid children," he told me. "Very bright and healthy. I don't believe you told me much about your husband?"

"I've never been married," I said, again shrieking with laughter, against my will. God, I would learn how to act refined, beginning tomorrow, if it was the last thing I ever did. "They're all LOVE children, Mr. Klausmeyer." He sat so straight and earnest and looking so sophisticated I had to postpone my graduation from kindergarten for at least another minute. And then I had that awful sinking sensation, knowing I'd behaved like a perfect fool. As of course I was. Nobody knew that better than I did. But Mr. Klausmeyer was so perfect, I wondered if he could possibly know it. Probably not. Perfect people never understand much about anything.

"Excuse me, Mr. Klausmeyer, if I confide in you. I've never done it before. There's something about you *Factways* people that seems to invite all kinds of confidences."

I suppose this lie was just too transparent, for he said nothing at all, and a moment later we were getting out of the cab, Mr. Klausmeyer looking just too pleased and preoccupied for words because he would soon be rid of me. God damn him. If I'd been dressed when he arrived, if I'd really wanted to make an impression, I could have had

him under my thumb in five seconds. But who wanted to
have an angleworm under her thumb?

I was drunk and sedate for the whole three minutes it
took us to enter the building and ride up in the elevator.
Dignity was a game two could play at. But after I'd used
up mine, and we got out of the elevator, I asked: "Just
what am I supposed to do, Mr. Klausmeyer? Besides collect a hundred dollars?"

Of course, without meaning to, I'd cut loose with another raucous laugh.

"Don't worry about your hundred dollars," he said,
shortly. "The man who bought your picture is somewhere
in this building. It is just a question of time, until we locate him. All you have to do is identify him when we
do locate him."

I was suddenly awfully sick of Mr. Klausmeyer, the detectives who'd been questioning me, and the whole insane
affair. What business was it of mine, all of this? I had just
one business in life, to paint pictures. If other people got
pleasure out of destroying them, let them; perhaps that was
the way they expressed their own creative instincts. They
probably referred to the best ones they suppressed or
ruined as their outstanding masterpieces.

It was a black thought, and I knew it was not in the
right perspective. As Mr. Klausmeyer put his hand on the
knob of an office door, and pushed it open, I said: "You
must be a dreadfully cynical and sophisticated person, Mr.
Klausmeyer. Don't you ever long for a breath of good,
clean, wholesome, natural fresh air?"

He gave me a polite, but emotional glare.

"I've always avoided being cynical," he said. "Up until
now."

We entered a room filled with a lot of other office angle-worms.

"How many children have you got, Mr. Klausmeyer?" I asked, intending to speak in a low voice, but evidently I was yelling, because a lot of people turned around and looked at us.

"Two," he whispered, but it sounded like he was swearing. Then he put on a smile and brought me forward. But as I crossed the room, and looked around it, my attention was abruptly centered upon a picture on the wall. It was one of mine. *Study in Fury*. It was amazing. I could hardly believe it. "George," Mr. Klausmeyer was saying, "this is Miss Patterson, the artist." It was beautifully framed, too. "Miss Patterson, this is George Stroud, who has charge of our investigation. She's agreed to stay here until we have the man we want. She can give us some help, I believe."

A good-looking angleworm got up in back of a desk and came forward and shook hands with me.

"Miss Patterson," he said. "This is an unexpected pleasure."

I looked at him, and started to bellow, but lost my breath. Something was quite mad. It was the murderer, the very same man who bought the picture in the Third Avenue junkshop.

"How d'you do?" I said. I turned to Mr. Klausmeyer, but Mr. Klausmeyer just looked tired and relieved. I stared back at Mr. Stroud. "Well," I said, uncertainly, "what can I do for you?"

For the fraction of a second we looked at each other with complete realization. I knew who he was, and he knew that I knew. But I couldn't understand it, and I hesitated.

This ordinary, bland, rather debonair and inconsequential person had killed that Delos woman? It didn't seem possible. Where would he get the nerve? What would he know about the terrible, intense moments of life? I must be mistaken. I must have misunderstood the whole situation. But it was the same man. There was no doubt about it.

His eyes were like craters, and I saw that their sockets were hard and drawn and icy cold, in spite of the easy smile he showed. I knew this, and at the same time I knew no one else in the room was capable of knowing it, because they were all like poor Mr. Klausmeyer, perfect.

"It's very kind of you to help us," he said. "I imagine Don explained what we're doing."

"Yes." My knees were suddenly trembling. This was away over my head, all of it. "I know everything, Mr. Stroud. I really do."

"I don't doubt it," he said. "I'm sure you do."

Why didn't somebody do something to break this afternoon nightmare? Of course it was a nightmare. Why didn't somebody admit it was all a stupid joke? What fantastic lie would this Stroud person invent, plausible as all hell, if I chose to identify him here and now?

I gave an automatic, raucous laugh, yanked my hand away from his, and said: "Anyway, I'm glad somebody likes my *Study in Fury*."

"Yes, I like it very much," said the murderer.

"It's yours?" I squeaked.

"Of course. I like all of your work."

There were about five people in the office, though it seemed more like fifty, and now they all turned to look at the *Fury*. Mr. Klausmeyer said: "I'll be damned. It really is Miss Patterson's picture. Why didn't you tell us, George?"

He shrugged.

"Tell you what? What is there to tell? I liked it, bought it, and there it is. It's been there for a couple of years."

Mr. Klausmeyer looked at the Stroud person with renewed interest, while the rest of them gaped at me as though for the first time convinced I was an artist.

"Would you care for a drink, Miss Patterson?" the murderer invited me. He was actually smiling. But I saw it was not a smile, only the desperate imitation of one.

I swallowed once, with a mouth that was harsh and dry, then I couldn't help the feeble, half-measure of a roar that came out of me. Even as I laughed, I knew I wasn't laughing. It was plain hysteria.

"Where in hell's my *Study in Fundamentals?*" I demanded. "The one your lousy magazine calls *Judas*."

Stroud was very still and white. The others were only blank. Mr. Klausmeyer said, to Stroud: "I told her we'd try to get the picture back for her." To me, he patiently explained, "I didn't say we had it, Miss Patterson. I meant that we'd automatically find the picture when we found the man."

"Will you?" I said, looking hard at Stroud. "I think more likely it's been destroyed."

Something moved in that rigid face of his, fixed in its casual, counterfeit smile.

"No," he said, at last. "I don't think so, Miss Patterson. I have reason to believe your picture is quite safe." He turned back to his desk and lifted the phone. Holding it, he gave me a hard, uncompromising stare it was impossible for me to misconstrue. "It will be recovered," he told me. "Provided everything else goes off all right. Do you fully understand?"

"Yes," I said. God damn him. He was actually blackmailing me. It was me who should be blackmailing him.

In fact, I would. "It damn well better be safe. I understand it's worth thousands and thousands of dollars."

He nodded.

"We think so. Now, what would you like to drink?"

"She likes muscatel," said Mr. Klausmeyer.

"Rye," I yelled. What did I care why he killed her? If the *Fury* was safe, probably the *Fundamentals* was safe, too, and it actually was worth a lot of money—now. And if it wasn't safe, I could always talk up later. Besides, he really did collect my pictures. "Not just one. A whole lot. Order a dozen."

It would take something to stay in the same room with a murderer. And at the same time remember that dignity paid, at least in public.

GEORGE STROUD X

Sometime very early I woke on a couch I'd had moved into my office, put on my shoes and necktie, the only clothing I'd removed, and in a mental cloud moved over to my desk.

My watch said a few minutes after eight. Today was the day. I still didn't know how I would meet it. But I knew it was the day. The police would finish the check-up in Albany. Somebody would think of combing the building.

Yesterday should have been the day, and why it wasn't, I would never really know. When that Patterson woman walked in here I should have been through. I knew why she hadn't identified me, the fact that I had not destroyed her picture, and my threat that I still would, if she opened her mouth. Artists are curious. I shuddered when I thought how close I'd come, actually, to getting rid of that canvas. She could still make trouble, any time she felt like it, and maybe she would. She was erratic enough. At about eight in the evening she'd packed herself off. But she might be back. At any moment, for any reason, she might change her mind.

Nobody answered when I pressed the button for a copy boy, and at last I phoned the drugstore downstairs. Eventually I got my sandwich and my quart of black coffee. In Roy's office, Harry Slater and Alvin Dealey were keeping the death watch.

Shortly before nine the rest of the staff began to come in. Leon Temple arrived, and then Roy, Englund, and Don and Eddy reached the office almost simultaneously.

"Why don't you go home?" Roy asked me. "There's nothing you can do now, is there?"

I shook my head. "I'm staying."

"You want to be in at the finish?"

"Right. How's everything downstairs?"

Leon Temple said: "Tighter than a drum. Phil Best has just spelled Mike. We've got the whole night side of the Van Barth down there, and some more special cops. I don't understand it."

This was it. I felt it coming. "What don't you understand?" I asked.

"Why that guy hasn't come out. What the hell. He's here, but where is he?"

"Maybe he left before we threw a line around the place," I said.

"Not a chance."

"He may have simply walked in one door and out the other," I argued. "Perhaps he knew he was being followed."

"No," said Leon. "That porter followed him right to the elevator. He took an express. He could be anywhere above the eighteenth floor. For all we know, he's somewhere up here in our own organization."

"What can we do about it?" Englund asked.

"He'll show," I said.

"I thought time was essential, George," Roy reminded me.

"It is."

"It occurs to me," said Leon, "if he doesn't show—" So it was going to be Leon Temple. I looked at him and waited. "We could take those eyewitnesses, with the building police, and some of our own men, and go through the whole place from top to bottom. We could cover every office. That would settle it. It would take a couple of hours, but we'd know."

I had to appear to consider the idea. It already looked bad that I hadn't suggested it myself. I nodded, and said: "You have something."

"Well, shall we do it?"

If I knew where those eyewitnesses were, if I could be informed of their progress from floor to floor and from suite to suite, there might still be a way. No game is over until the whistle blows.

"Get started," I said. "You handle this, Leon. And I want you to keep me informed of every move. Let me know what floor you start on, which direction you're working, and where you're going next."

"O.K.," he said. "First, we'll get witnesses and cops on every floor above eighteen. They'll cover the stairs, the elevators, and I'll have them be careful to watch people moving from office to office, the mail-chutes, johns, closets—everything." I nodded, but didn't speak. "I think that would be right, don't you?"

God, what a price. Here was the bill, and it had to be paid. Of course this was whining, but I knew no man on earth ever watched his whole life go to bits and pieces, carrying with it the lives of those close to him also down into ashes, without a silent protest. The man who really accepts his fate, really bows without a quiver to the big gamble he has made and lost, that is a lie, a myth. There is no such man, there never has been, never will be.

"All right," I said. "Keep me informed."

"I'd like to take Dick and Eddy and Don. And some more, as soon as they come in."

"Take them."

"And I think those witnesses should be encouraged."

"Pay them. I'll give you a voucher." I signed my name to a cashier's form, leaving the amount blank, and tossed it to Leon. "Good hunting," I said, and I think I created a brief smile.

Pretty soon the office was empty, and then Leon called to say they were going through the eighteenth floor, with all exits closed and all down-elevators being stopped for inspection. There was just one way to go. Up.

I had a half-formed idea that there might be some safety in the very heart of the enemy's territory, Steve's or Earl's offices on the thirty-second floor, and I was trying to hit upon a way to work it when the phone rang and it was Steve himself. His voice was blurred and strained, and somehow bewildered, as he asked me to come up there at once.

In Hagen's office I found, besides Steve, Earl Janoth and our chief attorney, Ralph Beeman, with John Wayne, the organization's biggest stockholder, and four other editors. And then I saw Fred Steichel, M.E. of Jennett-Donohue. All of them looked stunned and slightly embarrassed. Except Steichel, who seemed apologetic, and Earl, who radiated more than his customary assurance. He came forward and heartily shook my hand, and I saw that the self-confidence was, instead, nervous tension mounting to near hysteria.

"George," he said. "This makes me very glad." I don't think he really saw me, though, and I don't believe he saw, actually saw, anyone else in the room as he turned and went on, "I see no reason why we should wait. What I have to say now can be drawn up and issued to the entire staff later, expressing my regret that I could not have the pleas-

ure of speaking to each and every one of them personally."
I sat down and looked at the fascinated faces around me.
They sensed, as I did, the one and only thing that could
be impending. "As you may know, there have been certain
differences' on our controlling board, as to the editorial
policies of Janoth publications. I have consistently worked
and fought for free, flexible, creative journalism, not only
as I saw it, but as every last member of the staff saw it. I
want to say now I think this policy was correct, and I am
proud of our record, proud that I have enlisted the services
of so much talent." He paused to look at Hagen, who
looked at no one as he stonily concentrated upon a scramble
of lines and circles on the pad before him. "But the controlling board does not agree that my policies have been
for the best interests of the organization. And the recent
tragedy, of which you are all aware, has increased the op-
position's mistrust of my leadership. Under the circumstances, I cannot blame them. Rather than jeopardize the
future of the entire venture, I have consented to step aside,
and to permit a merger with the firm of Jennett-Donohue.
I hope you will all keep alive the spirit of the old organization in the new one. I hope you will give to Mr. Steichel,
your new managing editor, the same loyalty you gave to
Steve and myself."

Then the attorney, Beeman, took up the same theme and
elaborated upon it, and then Wayne began to talk about
Earl's step as being temporary, and that everyone looked
to his early return. He was still speaking when the door
opened and Leon Temple stepped inside. I went over to
him.

"We've drawn a blank so far," he told me. "But just to
be sure, I think we should go through both Janoth's and
Hagen's offices."

In the second that the door opened and shut, I saw a knot of people in the corridor, a porter from Gil's and a waiter from the Van Barth among them.

"Drop it," I said. "The assignment is killed."

Leon's gaze went slowly around the room, absorbing a scene that might have been posed in some historical museum. His eyes came back to me, and I nodded.

"You mean, send them all away?"

"Send them away. We are having a big change. It is the same as Pompeii."

Back in the room I heard Wayne say to Hagen: "—either the Paris bureau, or the Vienna bureau. I imagine you can have either one, if you want it."

"I'll think it over," Hagen told him.

"The organization comes ahead of everything," Earl was too jovially and confidently reiterating. It was both ghastly and yet heroic. "Whatever happens, that must go on. It is bigger than I am, bigger than any one of us. I won't see it injured or even endangered."

Our new managing editor, Steichel, was the only person who seemed to be on the sidelines. I went over to him.

"Well?" I said.

"I know you want more money," he told me. "But what else do you want?"

I could see he would be no improvement at all. I said: "Emory Mafferson."

I thought that would catch him off balance, and it did. "What? You actually want Mafferson?"

"We want to bring out Funded Individuals. In cartoon strips. We'll dramatize it in pictures." Doubt and suspicion were still there, in Steichel's eyes, but interest began to kindle. "Nobody reads, any more," I went on. "Pictorial presentation, that's the whole future. Let Emory go ahead with Funded Individuals in a new five-color book on slick paper."

Grudgingly, he said: "I'll have to think that one over. We'll see."

GEORGE STROUD XI

THE REST of that day went by like a motion picture running wild, sometimes too fast, and again too slow.

I called up Georgette, and made a date to meet her for dinner that evening at the Van Barth. She sounded extra gay, though I couldn't imagine why. I was the only member of the family who knew what it meant to go all the way through life and come out of it alive.

I explained that the last assignment was over, and then she put Georgia on the wire. The conversation proceeded like this:

"Hello? Hello? Is that you, George? This is George."

"Hello, George. This is George."

"Hello."

"Hello."

"Hello? Hello?"

"All right, now we've said hello."

"Hello, George, you have to tell me a story. What's her name?"

"Claudia. And she's at least fifteen years old."

"Six."

"Sixteen."

"Six. Hello? Hello?"

"Hello. Yes, she's six. And here's what she did. One day she started to pick at a loose thread in her handkerchief, and it began to come away, and pretty soon she'd picked her handkerchief until all of it disappeared and before she knew it she was pulling away at some yarn in her sweater, and then her dress, and she kept pulling and pulling and before long she got tangled up with some hair on her head and after that she still kept pulling and pretty soon poor Claudia was just a heap of yarn lying on the floor."

"So then what did she do? Hello?"

"So then she just lay there on the floor and looked up at the chair where she'd been sitting, only of course it was empty by now. And she said, 'Where am I?' "

Success. I got an unbelieving spray of laughter.

"So then what did I do? Hello? Hello?"

"Then you did nothing," I said. "Except you were always careful after that not to pull out any loose threads. Not too far."

"Hello? Is that all?"

"That's all for now."

"Good-bye. Hello?"

"We said hello. Now we're saying good-bye."

"Good-bye, good-bye, good-bye, good-bye."

After that I phoned an agency and got a couple of tickets for a show that evening. And then, on an impulse, I phoned the art dealer who had sent us the photograph of the Louise Patterson exhibit. I told him who I was, and asked: "How much are Pattersons actually worth?"

"That all depends," he said. "Do you want to buy, or have you got one you want to sell?"

"Both. I want a rough evaluation."

"Well. Frankly, nobody knows. I suppose you're referring to that recent article in your *Newsways?*"

"More or less."

"Well. That was an exaggeration, of course. And the market on somebody like Patterson is always fluctuating. But I'd say anything of hers would average two or three thousand. I happen to have a number of canvases of hers, exceptional things, you could buy for around that figure."

"What would the *Judas* bring? I mean the one with the hands. You sent us a photograph of it."

"Well, that's different. It's received a lot of publicity, and I suppose that would be worth a little more. But, unfortunately, I haven't got the picture itself. It is really lost, apparently."

"It isn't lost," I said. "I have it. How much is it worth?"

There was a perceptible wait.

"You actually have it?"

"I have."

"You understand, Mr. —"

"Stroud. George Stroud."

"You understand, Mr. Stroud, I don't buy pictures myself. I simply exhibit pictures, and take a commission from the sales made through my gallery. But if you really have that *Judas* I believe it can be sold for anywhere between five and ten thousand dollars."

I thanked him and dropped the phone.

The big clock ran everywhere, overlooked no one, omitted no one, forgot nothing, remembered nothing, knew nothing. Was nothing, I would have liked to add, but I knew better. It was just about everything. Everything there is.

That afternoon Louise Patterson came roaring into the office, more than a little drunk. I had been expecting her. She wanted to talk to me, and I packed us both off to Gil's.

When we were lined up at the bar at Gil's she said: "What about that picture of mine. What have you done with it?"

"Nothing. I have it at my home. Why should I have done anything with it?"

"You know why," she thundered. "Because it proves you killed Pauline Delos."

Three customers looked around with some interest. So then I had to explain to her that I hadn't, and in guarded language, suppressing most of the details, I outlined the police theory of the case. When I had finished, she said, disappointedly: "So you're really not a murderer, after all?"

"No. I'm sorry."

A cyclone of laughter issued from her. For a moment she couldn't catch her breath. I thought she'd fall off her chair.

"I'm sorry, too, Mr. Stroud. I was being so brave yesterday afternoon in your office, you have no idea. God, what I won't do to save those pictures of mine. The more I saw you the more sinister you looked. Come to think of it, you really are sinister. Aren't you?"

She was quite a woman. I liked her more and more. Yesterday she'd looked like something out of an album, but today she'd evidently taken some pains to put herself together. She was big, and dark, and alive.

Gil ranged down the bar in front of us.

"Evening," he said to both of us, then to me, "Say, a friend of yours was hanging around here for the last week or so, looking for you. He sure wanted to see you. Bad. But he ain't here now. A whole lot of people been looking for you."

"I know," I said. "I've seen them all. Give us a couple of rye highballs, and let the lady play the game."

Then for a while Gil and the Patterson woman worked away at it. She started by asking for a balloon, which was easy, the only toy Gil had saved from the old fire next to the carbarns, and ended by asking for a Raphael, also quite simple, a postcard he'd mailed to his wife from Italy, on a long voyage.

Something like eight drinks later Patterson remembered something, as I'd known she sooner or later would.

"George, there's something I don't understand. Why did they want me to identify you? What was the idea?"

She was more than a little drunk, and I gravely told her: "They wanted to find out who had that picture of yours. It was believed lost. Remember? And it's priceless. Remember that? And naturally, our organization wanted to trace it down."

She stared for a moment of semi-belief, then exploded into another storm of laughter.

"Double-talk. I want the truth. Where's my picture? I want it back. I could have it back the minute you were found, according to Mr. Klausmeyer." The memory of Don seemed to touch off another wave of deafening hilarity. "That angleworm. To hell with him. Well, where is it?"

"Louise," I said.

"It's worth a lot of money, it belongs to me, and I want it. When are you going to give it to me?"

"Louise."

"You're a double-talker. I can spot a guy like you a hundred miles away. You've got a wife, no children, and a house you haven't paid for. Tonight you're slumming, and tomorrow you'll be bragging all over the commuter's special that you know a real artist, the famous Louise Patterson." She slammed a fist on the bar. Gil came back to us and phlegmatically assembled two more drinks. "But to hell with all that. I want my *Study in Fundamentals*. It was promised to me, and it's worth a lot of money. Where is it?"

"You can't have it," I said, bluntly. "It's mine."

She glared, and snarled.

"You bastard, I think you mean it."

"Certainly I mean it. After all, it is mine. I paid for it, didn't I? And it means something to me. That picture is a part of my life. I like it. I want it. I need it."

She was, all at once, moderately amiable.

"Why?"

"Because that particular picture gave me an education. It is continuing to give me an education. Maybe, sometime, it will put me through college." I looked at my watch. If I could get to the Van Barth in ten minutes, I would be approximately on time. "But I'll make a deal with you. I've got that *Fury* in the office, and four other things of yours at home. You can have them all, instead of the *Temptation of St. Judas,* which is not for sale at any price. Not to anyone."

She asked me, wistfully: "Do you really like it so much?"

I didn't have time to explain, and so I simply said: "Yes."

This shut her up, and I somehow got her out of the place. In front of Gil's I put her into a cab, and paid the driver, and gave him her address.

I caught the next taxi that passed. I knew I'd be a few minutes late at the Van Barth. But it didn't seem to matter so much.

The big, silent, invisible clock was moving along as usual. But it had forgotten all about me. Tonight it was looking for someone else. Its arms and levers and steel springs were wound up and poised in search of some other person in the same blind, impersonal way it had been reaching for me on the night before. And it had missed me, somehow. That time. But I had no doubt it would get around to me again. Inevitably. Soon.

[174]

I made sure that my notebook was stowed away in an inside pocket. It had Louise's address, and her phone number. I would never call her, of course. It was enough, to be scorched by one serious, near-disaster. All the same, it was a nice, interesting number to have.

My taxi slowed and stopped for a red light. I looked out of the window and saw a newspaper headline on a corner stand.

EARL JANOTH, OUSTED PUBLISHER, PLUNGES TO DEATH.

TITLES IN SERIES